KRISTA'S DUTY

GEMMA JACKSON

POOLBEG

This book is a work of fiction. The names, characters, places, businesses, organisations and incidents portrayed in it are either the product of the author's imagination or are used fictitiously. Any resemblance to actual persons, living or dead, events or locales is entirely coincidental.

Published 2022
by Poolbeg Press Ltd.
123 Grange Hill, Baldoyle,
Dublin 13, Ireland
Email: poolbeg@poolbeg.com

© Gemma Jackson 2022

The moral right of the author has been asserted.

© Poolbeg Press Ltd. 2022, copyright for editing, typesetting, layout, design, ebook

A catalogue record for this book is available from the British Library.

ISBN 978178199-470-2

All rights reserved. No part of this publication may be reproduced or transmitted in any form or by any means, electronic or mechanical, including photography, recording, or any information storage or retrieval system, without permission in writing from the publisher. The book is sold subject to the condition that it shall not, by way of trade or otherwise, be lent, resold or otherwise circulated without the publisher's prior consent in any form of binding or cover other than that in which it is published and without a similar condition, including this condition, being imposed on the subsequent purchaser.

www.poolbeg.com

Also by Gemma Jackson

Through Streets Broad and Narrow
Ha'penny Chance
The Ha'penny Place
Ha'penny Schemes
Impossible Dream
Dare to Dream
Her Revolution

THE *KRISTA* SERIES OF NOVELLAS

Krista's Escape
Krista's Journey
Krista's Choice
Krista's Chance
Krista's Dilemma
Krista's Doubt
Krista's Duty

Published by Poolbeg

Foreword

Dear Reader,

This book opens in 1939. Hitler has begun his march to take over the world, though people in Europe are still praying for peace.

Krista and others like her who had one foreign parent could not join the services but they found ways to serve. I have read so many factual books – the private memoirs of individuals who served – that are being published these days, now that people are allowed to talk about their war service. These books make for fascinating and astounding reads. I read these books for my pleasure as well as research.

Krista joins women under the direct command of a rear admiral. She and the other women who form this group, for one reason or another, cannot openly join any of the services. I loosely based this group on real-life women who served in the Wrens (WRNS) as a daring group that became known as Freddie's Fairies. Freddie's Fairies began their work in 1940 so I have brought the story forward a year for my purposes. Information about these women is hard to come by but you will find mention of them in the accounts of others. I was riveted by what I found out about their work.

Freddie's Fairies mapped the coast of England, Scotland, Northern Ireland and Wales, discovering places to mount radio towers. They did not travel on motorcycles (as in my story) but in vans and under very difficult conditions. To my knowledge, no books have been written about them but I have found mention in many different places.

The training of all women during WWII was difficult. They were heckled and jeered at. It was very much 'keep them in their place'. Not only did they have to learn everything the men learned but had to overcome difficulties that the men never faced. Some of the 'tricks' played on women were particularly nasty, with the men in charge turning a blind eye. But they persevered – and they won their place in history. I was horrified to learn that even as late as 1970 serving sailors were told they should salute commanding Wren Officers only if they felt like it!

Krista's war is just beginning. Who knows where it will lead her? I certainly don't. So let us take this journey together and enjoy what I hope will be a darn good read.

Gemma

Chapter 1

Reserved Railway Carriage
London to Portsmouth
June 1939

"*Ladies!*" Hildegard Henderson stood with her legs braced and stared in abject horror at the women packed into both sides of the reserved railway carriage. She pulled at her restricting clothing, longing for a moment to herself. She was squeezed so tightly into her old Wren uniform – taken out of mothballs for the occasion – that it was difficult to breathe. Still, she had a duty to perform and she was a woman who never failed in her duties.

She stifled a sigh, looking out at the sea of lace and ribbons before her. What had head office been thinking of to send her such flibbertigibbets! She needed naval officers not debutantes. She forgot that she too had once been an over-excitable young woman.

"*Ladies!*" she shouted once more. "*Your attention, please – ladies!*"

Krista was pressed into her window seat, to one side of the long carriage. Her space and view of the opposite row of seats was blocked by an overlarge suitcase someone had dumped onto the seat beside her. She felt sorry for the poor woman sweating and shouting at the front of the carriage. She herself appeared to be the only one paying any attention to the woman. Then she saw her take something from her pocket and put it to her lips.

An ear-shattering whistle sounded, its piercing tones bringing silence finally to the carriage.

"I say," someone muttered, "there was no need to deafen us – a simple request would have sufficed."

"A bosun's whistle." Hildegard displayed the silver object in her hand. "You will soon get used to it." She hung the whistle by a silver chain over her head, struggling to get the chain over and around her tricorne hat. "My name is Hildegard Henderson and I have been put in charge of you sorry lot."

She marched along the cluttered aisle, holding on to the back of seats and sniffing in disgust at their occupants.

"You were all ..." and here she swung around to throw one arm dramatically about, "*all* given precise instructions as to what you could bring with you. It would appear that most of you have disregarded your written orders. It will be the last time you fail to obey." She glared. "*I assure you.*"

The women in the carriage looked uneasily at each other but remained silent.

"The train journey from London to Portsmouth is a long one. We could be aboard this train for up to eight hours!" She rammed her fist into the side of the huge suitcase sitting in the seat beside Krista, almost cutting off her breath.

"Excuse me!" Krista waved one hand over the top of the suitcase. "I have little enough room here as it is. I am having difficulty breathing. Could you refrain from pressing me further, please?"

"Oh, we have a fragile little flower here, do we?" Hildegard went onto the tips of her toes to see over the suitcase. "A foreign flower too, if I am not mistaken."

"Krista Lestrange, Miss Henderson." Krista was sorry she'd spoken out. The woman staring down at her was quite fearsome-looking. "The suitcase is not mine and it is taking up an inordinate amount of space as you can clearly see."

"I haven't time to speak to you." Hildegard turned away. "But this suitcase," and here she tapped the offending item, "is one of the many reasons I wish to address you motley crew."

She walked to the front of the carriage again. When she was sure she had everyone's attention she continued.

"You were all given an itemised list of what you could bring with you." She tried not to grind her teeth. "By the time this train has reached Portsmouth every single one of you will have repacked your luggage. Any items not on the order list will be sent back to your homes." She raised her voice to shout over the many objections being voiced. "*At your own expense! We will arrive in Portsmouth ready to move on to the next step of our journey. Have I made myself clear?*" She waited but when silence greeted her she shouted, "*Have I made myself clear?*"

"You cannot possibly expect us to survive with the ridiculous amount of luggage stated on that list, surely?" Andorra Prendergast stood to address the silly woman acting like a boarding-school headmistress. Did she expect them to respond with 'Yes. Miss'? They were adults. "It is my understanding that we could be in Portsmouth for months. The luggage I have with me will barely suffice."

There were mumblings of agreement from the women surrounding her.

"You have – *all of you* – volunteered to serve in the Women's Royal Naval Service – the Wrens." Hildegard looked around her in despair. When news of this fiasco got out – and it would – they would be laughingstocks in Portsmouth. Laughingstocks! It didn't bear thinking about.

"Yes, of course." Andorra continued to stand, smiling brightly as she fluffed her brown hair. "One wants to do one's duty for one's country, of course. But I volunteered to be an officer. I won't be marching around all over the place saluting!" She laughed gaily.

"Might I suggest that you collect your luggage at

the next train station and return home?" Hildegard would be glad to see the back of that one. She'd been trouble from the very first moment. She knew her type.

"Don't be ridiculous. I couldn't bear to miss all the fun." Andorra gave another of her tinkling laughs.

"Fun!" Hildegard had no more time to waste on this woman. She had matters to attend to. "Who does this belong to?" She was once more standing in the aisle by Krista.

"*It's mine, miss!*" a fluttery voice called.

"Stand up when you address me." Hildegard swung on her heel to find the owner of the voice. "State your name."

"Eugenie Carpenter, miss."

Hildegard stared at the short, brown-eyed blonde waving a limp arm in her direction. Surely this one did not meet the minimum height restrictions? She would be checking that as a matter of urgency. There were twenty-two women in this carriage. Would the Wrens get even eight possible officers from this lot? They would have their work cut out for them.

"*Sit.*" Hildegard closed her eyes in despair. First things first. "Would the women who obeyed their written orders – *to the letter, mind* – please stand up?" She sighed when only five of the women stood. "You five, step into the aisle, on the double."

Krista looked at the large case sitting in the seat beside her. How on earth was she going to get around that thing? It appeared as if it might weigh more than she did. She knew better than to ask for help from the disagreeable woman who appeared to be in charge of them. She stood with the others and with a deep breath put the long strap of her bag across her body. She climbed onto the seat with a grimace of distaste – but what could she do? The large suitcase was blocking her exit unless she dropped to the floor and crawled under the behemoth. She threw one silk-clad leg over the bulk of the case and used the toe of her shoe to seek blindly for the padded armrest that was keeping the suitcase in position. She put her hands on the body of the suitcase and, using it for balance, with a yell swung her other leg over the case, landing with bent knees on her feet in the aisle. She made a frantic examination of her stockings. She wanted to clap her hands and laugh. The twins would be so proud of her. She was unaware of the woman bearing down on her.

"You are one of Reggie's lot." Hildegard wanted to laugh. The girl had shown initiative. Shame she wouldn't cut the mustard as a Wren.

"I am not familiar with the term, miss."

"There should be three of you." Hildegard, ignoring the remark, marched back down the train and grabbed her clipboard from the stacked shelving unit bolted to the wall of the carriage. Checking it, she turned. "*Gerda Mullins!*" she shouted.

"*Here, miss!*" A plump woman waved.

Hildegard was not surprised to see that the woman was among those standing in the aisle who had packed as ordered. Reggie knew how to pick them.

"*Elaine Greenwood!*"

"*Here, miss!*" A black-haired beauty, also standing in the aisle, waved.

"I have a note here that states you three are on special assignment under the command of Rear Admiral Reginald Andrews." Hildegard waved at the five women. "All of you move into the dining carriage while I get this lot sorted out. You three," she pointed to Krista, Elaine and Gerda, "take the time to get to know each other. You will be spending a great deal of time together."

Krista joined the women moving in the direction of the dining car. She had been fascinated to learn she was not the only one ordered onto this train by Violet Andrews' brother.

The two women who had not been named moved deep into the dining carriage while Krista joined the other two who stood waiting by a dining booth.

"I am Krista Lestrange, also under the command of Rear Admiral Andrews," she introduced herself when the plump woman stepped up to the booth.

"Gerda Mullins."

"Hello, you two!" The third member of their little group joined them. "I am Elaine Greenwood."

They quickly slid onto the leather seats on each side of a narrow table bolted to the carriage floor. Krista sat on one side with Gerda Mullins, Elaine Greenwood facing them.

"I had no idea there would be others here under the rear admiral's command," Elaine leaned forward to say softly. "Did you?"

The other two shook their heads.

"Do you have any idea what we are doing here?" Elaine asked.

"I believe I was chosen because of my language skills," Krista offered.

"Me too." Gerda nodded her head frantically, happy to discover that she had something in common with these two elegant beauties. "I was my German grandmother's nurse for many years. Grossmutti would only speak German in her final years. I was working in my uncle's pawnshop when men came around our neighbourhood seeking people with language skills. My German is fluent but my French needs work. I am not in a position to volunteer for the services."

"My father is a royal naval captain but Mama is French," Elaine said. "My family spend all of our holidays at the home of my maternal grandparents in the south of France. I had thought to seek employment with one of the many fashion magazines in Paris but my father wouldn't hear of it. In my case, my French is fluent but my German needs work." She leaned in closer, not wishing to be overheard by the waiter she could see approaching. "Do you really believe that is why we have been chosen for this – whatever this is?"

"We can but wait and see," Krista said as the waiter stepped up to their table.

"Ladies!" The young man made a visual examination of the women. He'd taken his time strolling down the length of the carriage to this lot. He wanted to hear as much as possible of what they were talking about before he reached the table. He'd seen them being separated from that silly herd of females. He'd also heard the scuttlebutt about a special force Rear Admiral Andrews had dreamed up.

"Before we order," Krista leaned around Gerda to say, "can you tell us, please – how is the coffee?"

"We serve percolated ground coffee, miss," the waiter assured her. "I don't drink it myself but I have been told it is excellent."

"Thank you." Krista smiled up at the waiter. "I will have coffee."

"I too will have coffee," said Gerda.

"Tea for me, please," Elaine said with a smile.

The waiter went to carry out their order.

Before the other two could speak, Elaine held up a finger for silence.

She stepped out into the aisle and followed along in the waiter's wake without him noticing. She stood back as he pushed open a door at the other end of the carriage. She coughed politely and, while the waiter stood with his hand holding the door open revealing a kitchen station, she enquired after the train's restroom.

He directed her and she smiled her thanks.

She saw enough to be sure before turning on her heels and hurrying back to the others.

"Did either of you notice the insignia on the waiter's shirt?" she leaned in to demand softly as soon as she had taken her seat.

"I didn't," Krista said.

"Nor I," Gerda said.

"I wasn't sure before ..." Elaine gestured to her

companions to lean in. "Now I am. I kept my eyes open when we were on the railway platform before boarding. I noticed a number of naval men standing about smoking. I think the carriage we were assigned, plus the luggage carriage and this dining carriage are all under naval command. I find that fascinating. The men working in the kitchen and our waiter are all serving naval men. It would appear we are already under naval command. What do you think of that?"

"My mother was a Wren in the Great War ..." Krista cringed when she thought of the impression they must be giving to the men on board.

"As was mine," Gerda said.

Elaine shrugged, unsure what effect something like that could have on the present situation.

"My mother's old comrades in arms, so to speak, have been very active in reinstating the Wrens," Krista said. "They met with vehement opposition at every turn. Do you think it is possible that we are being observed and judged by the navy to see how this first lot of Wrens will fit in?"

"It wouldn't surprise me in the least." Elaine wished she could speak with her father. He'd be able to tell her what was what.

"If that is the case." Gerda said slowly, "I do not think we will have made a very good first impression."

"Why do you say that?" Krista had her own opinion but she preferred to keep it to herself.

"I was one of the first at the train station," Gerda said. "I have a terrible habit of always being early. It is most annoying ..."

"And?" Elaine prompted.

"I listened to the women speaking of ball gowns and dance shoes. They were most interested in meeting naval officers from what I could understand. I saw servants carrying mountains of matching luggage onto the platform." She shrugged. "Nothing I heard made me think of women preparing to serve their country."

The sound of raised voices carried into the dining car from the adjacent carriage. The waiter hurried to push open the doors that separated the two carriages.

Krista and Gerda leaned forward to see a sight that defied description. There were open suitcases littering the carriage and what appeared to be ball gowns being flung in all directions. Women were shouting and cursing. Two men hurried forward from the rear of the carriage where the kitchen was located. They joined the waiter, standing at his shoulders, and laughed at the struggling women.

Elaine was leaning out of her seat to have a better view of the chaos. "Well, you can't say we haven't made an impression!"

11

Chapter 2

"Well, that was fun." Andorra dropped heavily into the seat beside Elaine. She took her cigarettes from a pocket and offered the silver cigarette case around the table. When the other three refused, she lit a cigarette and blowing a stream of smoke examined the three women. "We will lose five of our number at the next train station. They refuse to stay."

"You were not tempted to leave?" Krista asked.

"Never!" Andorra clicked her manicured fingers at the waiter. "I am gasping for a cup of tea. The battle of the wardrobe was quite fatiguing."

She ordered tea from the attentive waiter.

"You've reorganised your luggage?" Gerda noticed

the woman's wrists and fingers were bare of jewellery.

"Oh, yes, the men in the luggage carriage are very efficient." Andorra puffed on her cigarette. "All jewellery was placed in a safe and will be returned to us when we leave Portsmouth at the end of our training. We filled out forms and labels to return our belongings to our homes. The trunks and whatnot will be unloaded with the ladies who are leaving us at the next station." She laughed gaily. "The goods will be sent COD – cash on delivery. Papa will be thrilled to pay the carriage duties, I'm sure! I had one of the luggage men hold that blasted list we were provided with while I packed my smallest suitcase." She shrugged. "How we are expected to survive with so little to hand, I do not know – but we shall see what we shall see, shall we not?"

The four women remained silent while the waiter placed cups and saucers, a jug of milk, a sugar bowl and a tea strainer on top of a slop bowl onto the table top. He left and returned with two silver pots in hand. "You ladies must be thirsty." He almost smirked. "Tea and coffee." He put the pots on the table. "Serve yourselves."

"Thank you." Andorra smiled sweetly. "Admiral Tennent assured me that his men were the best of the best."

There was a noticeable hitch in the waiter's stride when he walked away.

"Admiral Tennent?" Elaine asked as she poured tea from the silver pot.

"He is the Portsmouth commanding officer." Andorra accepted the cup of tea gratefully.

"You know him?" Krista poured coffee for Gerda and herself.

"Never met the man." Andorra left bright-red lipstick on the rim of her white cup. Her brown eyes laughed over the cup as she met Krista's eyes. "Name-dropping is such a useful tool. By the time this train reaches Portsmouth every man on these carriages will believe I am a personal friend of the admiral."

"Clever!" Elaine laughed.

"Now, tell me, what makes you so different that you are not members of our merry little group?" Andorra's eyes might sparkle but there was a keen intelligence at work.

"My father was French," Krista told the familiar lie. "I would not qualify to serve in the Wrens."

"My mother is French – same reason." Elaine shrugged.

"I cannot afford to work without a salary," Gerda said.

"So, why are you here?" Andorra almost demanded.

"To learn." Krista looked at Elaine and Gerda. "That is all we know at this point."

"Intriguing." Andorra stubbed out her cigarette before lighting another.

Gerda opened the window over her head.

"Old Henny seemed very impressed with you lot." Andorra wanted more information.

"Henny?" Elaine queried.

"Well, really," Andorra gave one of her tinkling laughs, "with a name like Hildegard Henderson, what else could she be called?"

***

The journey passed with the women chatting politely while the train travelled through the English countryside.

There was silence at the station where the five young women who had decided to return to their homes were helped from the train. Porters rushed to assist with the many cases and trunks unloaded.

They were served a delicious evening meal while the chatter continued.

It was dark when the train arrived in Portsmouth. The evening breeze and the sea air were welcome after the stuffy confines of the carriage and the clouds of smoke from the many smokers.

A large troop transport truck, its canvas sides tied down to protect against the inclement weather, was waiting for the women. They struggled to get themselves and their luggage into the high vehicle. There was much laughter, a few curses and helping female hands but finally they were all on board, sitting on wooden benches on both sides of the truck.

They were silent as they travelled along in darkness.

When the truck stopped, a hand rattled the canvas cover and a male voice shouted, "*Everybody out! Let's be having yeh!*"

The women struggled to exit the vehicle. Some wearing heels almost turned their ankles as they jumped down to the ground. They were herded along wet cobbles in the direction of a large grey stone building. When they reached the building, they were directed down stone steps to the lower floor where they were told to wait.

"Come along, ladies!" Hildegard Henderson pushed her way to the front.

She was quietly seething. The men had enjoyed the flash of stocking-tops while the women struggled to exit the truck. They had not offered to lend a hand. Surely there were wooden steps normally provided to exit a high vehicle? If she wasn't mistaken many of the electric lights were not lit. Someone was making their displeasure known. She sighed and led the women along the almost black corridor in the direction she had been given for their quarters.

She pushed open a door, stepped inside and beat her hand along the wall inside, looking for light switches. When she'd managed to find them and switch on the lights, she stared. Lines of metal beds marched down each side of a long bare room. Each bed had a naked thin grey striped mattress. A flat pillow and white sheets with grey woollen blankets were folded neatly at the foot of each bed.

"*Ladies, shut the drapes across those windows!*" Hildegard barked, conscious as she did so that she needed to start using naval terms like porthole for window, cabin for room, deck for floor and berth for bed as was directed in her orders. Later – she could take care of all of that later – right now she just wanted to spit!

The women were startled to see that there were grinning young male faces pressed up against the three tall windows that ran along one side of the room.

With the lights in the room on, the interior was well illuminated, much to the young men's delight.

Krista, Andorra and Eugenie shook off their shock the quickest and each moved to a window to draw the heavy drapes across the glass, ignoring the young men rapping on it, shouting rude comments and laughing.

Some of the women were standing in the open door, mouths agape, with the rest trailing out into the corridor.

"*Come inside, all of you!*" Hildegard stood in the centre aisle of the long room, staring around in disgust. "*Close the door!*"

"These beds don't appear to be secure." One of the women shook an iron bedframe. Her gentle shake almost rattled loose the screws holding the bed together. "Shoddy workmanship."

"Who are you?" Hildegard couldn't remember all of the names to go with the faces.

"Helen Benson, Miss Henderson," the woman answered while poking around in the bag tied across her chest. She was not very tall but the navy woollen dress she wore complimented her slim figure, and the defined muscular shape of her arms and legs showed a woman in top physical condition. She looked up, flipping her brown hair back, her brown eyes shining as she held something in a clenched fist. "I never leave home without my Swiss army knife!"

"Benson." Hildegard consulted the clipboard she'd held pressed to her heaving breast. "You are the rally driver, are you not?"

"I am, Miss Henderson." Helen opened the Swiss

army knife, selected a tool and got to work on the first of the beds. "If anyone else could help," she grunted as she tightened the loose screws. "There are rather a lot of beds."

"Well, ladies," Hildegard looked around vaguely, "is anyone else as prepared as Miss Benson?"

"*I have a metal nail file!*" a voice called.

"So have I!" several voices chorused.

"Right." Helen stood up. "If you can use your nail files to start to tighten the screws, I will come behind and use my tool to fully tighten them. Don't try to make them tight with the nail files because they will snap. If we put our minds to it, ladies, we should succeed in getting these beds fit for our use in no time."

"I have a Swiss army knife." Andorra stepped forward with a red-handled knife in her hand. "I can help tightening screws."

"Prendergast," Hildegard didn't have to consult her clipboard – this one was unmistakeable, "You are a yachtswoman, I believe."

"I am a championship yachtswoman. With silver cups to prove it." Andorra looked around the room. "There is no need to hide our lights under a bushel here. We are all in this together. From the welcome we have received it looks very much like it is to be Us against Them."

"I too have a Swiss army knife." Eugenie Carpenter threw off her jacket, revealing muscled arms. "I am a championship show jumper. I too have the cups and ribbons to prove it." She smiled shyly around the room. "I am accustomed to being underestimated."

"Capital!" Hildegard wanted to clap her hands in delight. The women were already pulling together. "If we could form teams with those who hold a Swiss army knife at the head of those with nail files, we will soon have this room set to rights."

"It's getting late." Elaine Greenwood stepped forward. "Perhaps we should elect a bed-making team. We can make the beds as each one is finished."

"Good idea," said Hildegard. "And while we are putting this room to rights, you should introduce yourselves." She wanted to encourage the team spirit.

She opened a door leading off the long room, switched on the light for a moment, sniffing when she discovered a room obviously meant as a lounge. It didn't offer a great deal of comfort. Another door opened into the hallway leading to a cold, white-tiled multiple-stall bathroom.

"I am Elaine Greenwood." Elaine stood tall and pressed a hand to her chest. "My father is a naval captain. I am to be under the direct command of Rear Admiral Andrews but I am delighted to be part of this group. I look forward to getting to know you ladies."

"I am Gerda Mullins. I too am under the command of Rear Admiral Andrews."

"I am Celine Cartwright," a tall slim blonde said. "I have experience of many types of sailing vessels." She smiled around, her green eyes sparkling. "I have no cups or medals, though – just older brothers I insisted on following after."

There were more introductions as the women worked.

It would be impossible to remember every name and occupation or skill-set but it lent a friendly atmosphere to the room while the women set to with a will.

By the time they had repaired and made the beds they were tired. They each selected a bed and, after unpacking only their needs for the night, it was time for lights out. They stacked their suitcases, still packed, on the floor at the foot of their beds. They washed without complaining in a room with large white sinks and cold running water. They drank from the taps. They had missed the last serving in the mess hall.

The following morning the sound of whistles and boat-horns woke the women. There was barely any light coming through the heavy curtains pulled across the windows. Elaine, whose bed was close to a window, leaned over to lift a tiny section of the curtain. "*Do not draw the curtains until we are washed, dressed and the room restored to order!*" she shouted while still in her bed. "*We have an interested audience outside!*"

"My grandmother always said 'it takes little to amuse little minds'," someone remarked in the semi-darkness.

"*Ladies, you heard Greenwood! Rise and shine!*" Hildegard felt as if she hadn't slept at all. She'd been forced by lack of a private cabin to sleep in the same room as the other women. "Come along now," she encouraged to a chorus of groans that greeted her words. "We will not be kept prisoner by some spotty-chinned young men with not a great deal to do with themselves." She knew the young midshipmen should have been about their business. Someone was turning a blind eye. She stifled her heavy sigh in her pillow.

There was a great deal of mumbling and grumbling while the women crawled or fell out of their beds. Those who managed to remain sleeping were shaken awake by their roommates.

There was a gathering of moaning, scratching, yawning women in the room set for their ablutions. They washed once more in cold water and returned to their long room to dress for the day.

Krista knew exactly what she would be wearing. It was a blessing not to have too much choice when you were awakened so early in the morning then forced to shuffle along with others to prepare for the day. She had packed two pairs of navy slacks. The choice between skirt or slacks had been offered in their written orders.

Some of the women were daring enough to stand naked by the sides of their beds but Krista wasn't one of them. She left her nightdress on while pulling on her knickers. She put knee-socks on before putting her legs into her slacks, then jumped around pulling the slacks up while fighting the folds of her nightdress. She shoved her feet into navy-blue leather walking shoes which she then laced up tightly. She had a short-sleeved white shirt and navy-blue cardigan to complete the outfit.

"Is everyone decent?" Hildegard, once more forced into her old Wren's uniform but without the jacket and hat, shouted.

She walked along the room to check that all of the women had left their beds. When she was assured it was safe, she went to one of the windows and pulled the drapes open herself.

She was ready, armed with her clipboard. She shoved up the bottom of the sash-window and shouted, "*You men are on charge! State your names!*" She held a pencil ready and watched the midshipmen disappear, showing their heels as they ran.

The women whistled and clapped at their leader's success.

Hildegard turned from the window. "Beds must be made, order restored to the room. But first stand by your beds while I inspect your attire."

The women promptly obeyed.

Hildegard tried not to close her eyes and shake her head. Some of the clothing being worn would blow in the always present sea breeze, providing delightful entertainment for the sailors.

"Miss Lestrange," Hildegard had just noticed Krista's clothing, "if you would step forward for a moment." She waited until a nervous-looking Krista stepped over to join her. "Ladies, if I could have your attention! Please make note of what Miss Lestrange is wearing."

She walked around Krista, waving her hand at each item she mentioned. "Her slacks, navy to match the uniform of the naval service. A sensible white blouse, a navy cardigan in case the weather cools. Make special note of her sensible walking shoes. She will be able to move without giving the staring sailors a glimpse of stocking-tops. Those of you wearing ridiculous high-heel shoes and floating dresses – *CHANGE.*"

"Teacher's pet." Andorra nudged Krista with her elbow. Since she was wearing an outfit almost identical to Krista's, there was no malice in the nudge.

Chapter 3

"Oh, you're lovely, you are!"

A hard shoulder-nudge almost sent Krista flying.

"What's your name, Fraulein? I couldn't take you home to meet me mam but never mind. Want to meet me outside for a smoke? We can get to know each other. Make friends not enemies." The young seaman grinned at Krista, delighted by the hooting yells of his mates.

"*This one won't need much feeding!*" another sailor shouted, poking a stiff finger into Eugenie Carpenter's shoulder. "*She's only bite-sized!*"

The women smiled politely through gritted teeth, determined not to be driven out of the NAAFI canteen. They were hungry and thirsty. They stood patiently with trays in hand, waiting to be served the sausage, beans and toast on offer by the men standing behind the counter.

"*That's enough, lads!*" an older man barked. "*You're holding up the line!*"

"Fit you women better to be standing back here cooking and cleaning!" a short male barked at Gerda as he threw a ladle of beans onto the thick white plate he held. "It's all you're good for!"

The women continued to ignore the heckling as they shuffled along the line to receive their food and drink. If they dropped their trays onto the long table they had commandeered for their group with more force than necessary, no one made mention of it. Those who sat with their backs to the room had hunched shoulders, waiting for a missile of some sort to be thrown at them.

Hildegard sighed at the verbal abuse that continued to be directed at her charges. It would appear nothing had changed – she had so hoped that in the years since the Great War the attitude to women in the services might have softened slightly.

"*Nooo!*" Celine Cartwright pushed her chair back, preparing to stand when she saw food being flung in their direction.

"*Here, you lot! I'll have none of that!*" A heavy-set man, wrapped in folds of white fabric, stepped out of the serving area onto the floor of the canteen. He had his back to the table where the women sat. "There will be no throwing of food under my watch. Wasteful, that's what that is. You lot should be ashamed of yourselves.

Now eat up and get out or next time I see your ugly faces you won't be served! *Do I make myself clear?*"

Chef Paul Young had seen what was going on in his canteen. He didn't approve. When he saw the sailors at the table closest to the females prepare spoons of beans to fling at the backs of the women, he knew he had to put a stop to it. He wouldn't allow such goings-on in his little kingdom.

"I hope none of you are on guns. You missed." Chef Young looked at the smashed beans in tomato sauce lying on the deck in disgust. "Perkins, get out here and clean up this deck."

A young man bucket and mop in hand hurried to join the chef.

"Stand watch over this area until I release you from duty." With that the chef returned to his kitchen.

"*Ladies!*" Hildegard practically shouted. The noise from the sailors grouped around tables in the cafeteria, and their shouting over each other amid the rattle of crockery and cutlery made a chore out of being heard by all at the table. "We have been placed under the command of Lieutenant McMasters. We will be meeting with him after breakfast." She consulted the notes attached to her clipboard – an article she never seemed to be without.

"What exactly are we doing here?" Andorra was keeping an eagle eye on the young ratings and able-bodied seamen around the room. The young lad ordered to clean the decking was standing still, leaning on his mop. From the looks of him, he was half asleep where he stood. "We have been jolly good sports, have we not? We were ordered to present ourselves without much explanation or direction. We even allowed our belongings to be returned to our homes, leaving us with practically nothing of our own for comfort. We are here now, being subjected to abuse from snot-nosed youngsters," She said this with all the dignity of her twenty-six years. "It would help if we knew what was expected of us."

"Hear, hear!" Helen Carpenter exclaimed with a nod towards Andorra.

There were nods of agreement from the others at the table.

"We will be here for six weeks, during which time you will receive a basic introduction to naval life," Hildegard said. "You will learn to march in formation." She leaned in and looked around the table. "I cannot stress enough the importance of our unit being able to present an efficient marching force when in company with other services." She flushed to remember the horror during the Great War when the Wrens were out of step while marching before His Majesty the King. The embarrassment remained with her to this day. She would not allow something like that to occur again.

There were gasps from many throats around the table.

"Marching?"

"I say!"

"No, really?"

"*We will learn to march in formation like a well-trained unit!*" Hildegard barked. "We will study Morse code, Navigation, Signalling, Shipboard Command and Etiquette. Some of us will learn to ride motorcycles."

"It would appear we are to return to school, ladies," Andorra said with a laugh. She had no need of lessons in sailing. She could, however, help the others.

"I was never very fond of the classroom." Helen shrugged.

"We will learn everything the Navy is willing to teach us." Hildegard drank the last of her cool tea, wishing for more but not willing to approach the serving counter again. "We will not just learn but excel. *Do I make myself clear?*"

"Yes, of course, dear." Andorra didn't like to see good old Henny so upset. "We will be everything you could wish." She pushed her chair back and stood. "Now, I want more tea – anyone else?"

Shouts of "Please!" and upheld cups answered her.

"Sit still." She waved a hand about when several of the women began to stand. "I'll bring a large pot of tea to the table." She walked off, then asked over her shoulder, "How are we for milk and sugar?"

"We could use more milk," a woman answered.

Andorra didn't know her name.

Andorra approached the counter and ordered a large pot of tea.

"There's no handing out of teapots here!" the same man who had barked at Gerda earlier snapped. "This isn't the Ritz, yeh know. You lot can come up for your tea just like everyone else."

"My good man," Andorra's cut-glass accent was pronounced as she glared down at the insubordinate server, "do you really believe that we are willing to subject ourselves to more of your abuse? The tea, please!" When he delayed in jumping to her command, she barked, "*Fetch your officer ... at once!*"

"What's going on here?" Chef Paul Young had heard the goings-on. He was busy overseeing the return to order of his kitchen and preparing for lunch and the snacks that would be on hand for people throughout the day. He didn't have time for this. He stifled a sigh. These women were going to be more trouble than they were worth. He just knew it.

"Who are you?" Andorra demanded.

"I am Chef Young," Paul answered to the note of command in her voice.

"Well, Chef Young, I am Andorra Prendergast – you may have heard of me – I have won the Henley Regatta with my yacht *Sunbeam* two years running?" She waited for him to absorb this impressive fact. "My companions and I are simply gasping for more tea." She glanced over her shoulder, aware she had caught the attention of the men sitting at their leisure around the room enjoying a smoke. "We didn't want to cause any more disturbance by approaching the serving line in a group. Would it be so difficult to brew a fresh pot of tea – a large pot – so that we can serve ourselves? Oh, and more milk, please."

"See to it, Walsh." Paul knew when he needed to comply.

"But, Chef!"

"*That is an order.*"

***

"I am going to throw that man overboard." Andorra shuffled in place, trying to relieve some of the pressure on her aching feet.

"I'll help," Helen Benson offered.

"The man is a sadist," Elaine Greenwood groaned.

"Shall we try that again, ladies?" Chief Petty Officer David Timmons, a slender figure in his immaculate uniform, wondered what he had done to deserve this posting. "Perhaps this time we could manage to march in a straight line. That shouldn't be too strenuous even for delicate flowers such as yourselves. Henderson, to the front ..."

The women continued to be drilled in the basics of marching in formation, much to the amusement of passing seamen.

It was a shambles – half the women didn't know their right foot from their left. Those who against all advice were wearing heels were wobbling and moaning.

The officers in charge of the able-bodied seamen training on the same grounds were grinning, turning a deaf ear to the salacious comments being shouted by the seamen at the sweating women.

"This is a fine mess, Chief." A tall broad-shouldered man had joined the Chief Petty Officer. His dark hair was cut close to his head, his pale eyes narrowed as he watched the women hobble and wobble around.

"I've seen worse," David Timmons said.

"Really?" Owen McMasters stared at his friend in disbelief.

"No, not really, but one can hope."

David Timmons turned to the women and in a loud voice commanded that they stop and come to attention. He wanted to close his eyes at the disaster waiting to happen. He was surprised to see that the women remained on their feet in spite of several smashing into the line in front of them.

"Henderson, form them up and follow!" Timmons shouted.

"Who is he?" Gerda Mullins jerked her chin in the direction of the tall good-looking officer.

"He's wearing the insignia of a lieutenant," Elaine Greenwood whispered.

Krista wanted to roll her eyes to heaven. The morning so far had been a disaster. Heaven alone knew what the men marching in step in front of them thought.

"He is quite the dish." Alice Newton, a sultry brunette, licked her lips and patted her hair while practically eating the tall lieutenant with her narrowed amber eyes.

"Those shoulders ..."

"I like a man with tight firm buttocks ..."

"I wonder what size shoes he wears ..."

The women giggled, each understanding the reference – it was said a man's private equipment could be judged by the size of the shoes he wore.

Owen McMasters tried not to blush at the comments being made about his physique.

"Silence in the ranks!" Timmons shouted, fighting the grin that wanted to stretch over his face.

Chapter 4

"Take a seat, ladies!" Chief Petty Officer Timmons held the door of a classroom open and barked at the women as they straggled along the corridor. "*Come along!* We do not have all day and there is much to be achieved!" He tried not to sigh aloud. He would need a strong drink before this day got very much older.

Owen McMasters walked to the front of the room, staring at the tall blackboard as if seeking inspiration. He turned when he heard the door closing at his back and addressed the room.

"I am Lieutenant McMasters. You may address me as 'lieutenant' or 'sir'. I will be in charge of your training. You have already met Chief Petty Officer Timmons …"

He gestured towards Timmons who was standing to one side of the door.

McMasters looked out over the women sitting behind the desks – desks formed of metal with wooden tops and seats – ranked along the width and length of the room. He kept his eyes firmly turned away from the flash of stocking-tops offered him through the open fronts of the desks by the bold females who had dared to hitch up their skirts as they sat.

"Henderson, why are this lot not in uniform?" he barked.

"*Sir*." Henny came to her feet, standing erect to one side of her desk at the front of the classroom, her ample bosom tightly bound, standing proud, arms by her sides. "The Powers That Be are deciding on the uniform as we speak."

McMasters eyes scanned the room. He stopped at Krista's bright white-blonde head. He knew who she was. It was impossible to miss those striking looks and Rear Admiral Andrews had made him aware of this woman and two others who had been granted a place within this first group of trainee Wrens.

"You!" He pointed a stiff finger at Krista. "Front and centre, on the double."

Krista stepped to the side, away from her desk. She walked with her head high and her tummy trembling towards the front of the room.

"This," McMasters walked around Krista before once more staring into the classroom at the rows of desks, "is an acceptable fashion of dressing until uniforms have been issued to you. For those of you not wishing to ape men and appear masculine by wearing slacks – a box-pleated skirt –" He glared at the titters his knowledge of ladies' fashion evoked. "I have sisters!" he snapped before returning his attention to Krista. "As I was saying before I was so rudely interrupted ... a box-pleated skirt to below the knee and thick serviceable stockings may be worn."

Groans of dismay greeted his words.

"You may return to your seat," he almost grunted towards Krista. He paid no more attention to her as he continued to speak. "We will have no more high heels and silk stockings. There will be no more flashing red lips and coy glances. This is not a bawdy house. You are in training and as such I expect you to look and behave like any other ratings on this ship. Do I make myself clear?"

"Yes, sir," came from several of the women.

"*Do I make myself clear?*" His loud demand almost rattled the classroom window.

"*Yes, sir!*" was shouted back at him from every throat and appeared to satisfy him.

A knock on the classroom door broke the heavy silence that fell after that.

"*Chief!*" McMasters snapped.

Timmons opened the door, revealing three men in naval uniform standing to attention outside.

"Permission to come aboard," the older man standing to the front of the threesome said.

"Granted," McMasters said.

"Oh my, this day just keeps getting better." Alice Newton's eyes gleamed at the sight of the three handsome men. "I do so admire a man in uniform. Why, it is quite like having a large box of delicious chocolates ... which to choose? What a delightful dilemma!"

McMasters almost groaned at the reaction of some of the women. How on earth was he supposed to handle raging hormones? No one had warned him of this problem when he was given his orders. "Ladies, Chief Timmons will be in charge of your physical training. Lieutenant Carey," the older man stepped forward at his name, "and Petty Officer Fox will be responsible for training you in radio handling and Morse code, additionally, I will be responsible for your conduct and naval deportment."

He didn't mention the other young man who had accompanied Lieutenant Carey into the room. Krista stared. It was Peregrine Fotheringham Carter attired in the uniform of a naval officer. She had to fight hard to keep her mouth from falling open and her eyes from popping out. What on earth was Perry doing here? And in naval uniform to boot! What was going on?

"Uniforms?" Carey grimaced at McMasters.

"Being decided upon apparently." McMasters shared a worried glance with his fellow-lieutenant.

"Something needs to be done about their attire."

The men were ignoring the women who were listening so avidly to every word.

"I had that discussion just before your arrival." McMasters had no idea what to do with this lot. He needed to have a discussion free of listening women. A plan needed to be formed for handling the latest headache the navy had given him.

"Henderson, if you could remain. The rest of you are dismissed. *Those of you who do not have suitable attire – get it! I want to see you all shipshape and Bristol fashion when you are on the parade ground tomorrow morning bright and early. Dismissed!*"

His words were greeted by groans as the women filed out of the room. Several took the time to throw coy glances towards the men. He made note of those. He would not allow such conduct to continue. They could shape up or ship out.

"We have not made a good showing so far, have we, Miss Henderson?" Elaine Greenwood, her blue eyes intense, almost whispered her question to Henny who was sitting at one end of the table in the NAAFI with her back to the kitchen and her eyes on the women.

There were teacups and ashtrays with clouds of smoke rising above them scattered along the table top. The sound of women exchanging groans and opinions was a soft murmur in the air. The cafeteria was almost devoid of men as the women had entered in a time between the hours set aside for meal service. There were a few sailors dotted around smoking, drinking tea and playing cards. They had grumbled when the women first appeared but were leaving them alone at the moment.

"We will do better or I will know the reason why." Henny checked the notes she had made on her clipboard.

Krista added nothing to the conversations going on

around the table. Her mind was ablaze with the shock of seeing Perry on this base – and in naval uniform. What could that mean?

"Miss Henderson, do you know why we have been included in this company?" Elaine pointed towards Krista and Gerda then towards herself. She knew it was wrong to point but how else was she to make herself clear? She needed to know what was expected of her. "All of this talk of marching and Morse code and naval regulations. Do we three really need to know all of this?"

"Greenwood," Henny, with a martyred sigh, turned her attention to the young woman, "your father is, I believe, a captain in His Majesty's navy?" She waited for Elaine's nod before continuing. "You will therefore be aware of naval rankings. We do not question our superior officers or their orders ... understood?" She didn't wait to see the woman's reaction but tapped the table top with her fountain pen to attract the attention of the women. "Wrens," she stared from one woman to the other, "it cannot surprise you to know that I am bitterly disappointed with our showing here today." She held up her hand when several of the women looked like objecting. "We discussed and, I believed, arranged matters concerning clothing while on the train that brought us here and again this morning. I simply cannot believe that any of you thought wearing sheer silk stockings, high-heeled shoes and floating skirts was in any way suitable to serve until such time as uniforms arrive for us." She closed her eyes briefly, trying not to see the bright lipstick and floating scarfs some of the women were wearing – even after this morning's fiasco. "Lestrange, who I happen to know is the youngest person here, has been held up as an example not once but twice today. Does that not make you ashamed of yourselves?" She waited to see if anyone would comment but they were all avoiding her eyes. "You were, all of you, chosen to take your place as leaders – officers – of the Wrens. We need women who can make us proud, not chattering flibbertigibbets! You have – all of you – earned individual awards in your fields of expertise, be it horse riding, yachting, motor rally. You have earned your stripes in the fields you chose to study. We need you to apply that determination to learning all that will be taught here." She slapped the tabletop, making the crockery rattle. "You are not here to select your latest paramour or nab a husband." She glared at Alice Newton when she said this. She had noticed the outrageous behaviour of the woman. Really, what had head office been thinking of, sending someone like that onto a male base?

"What do you want us to do?" Andorra Prendergast didn't like to see the poor woman swell and sweat in that unattractive manner.

"Prendergast, you are attired entirely suitably," Henny was forced to concede. "Could I have a show of hands – truthfully – of all of those who have the items they need to present themselves in a manner that will bring pride to the Wrens tomorrow morning? I have been informed that we have the rest of today to organise our affairs. Now – a show of hands – please!"

"I do not have thick stockings."

"I do not have walking shoes."

The list of 'do nots' echoed down the table.

"We will return to our cabin." Henny noticed the cafeteria beginning to fill up with hungry sailors who were giving far too much attention to the women. "Follow me – on the double."

"Wrens, enter quickly!" Henny's voice was choked as she held open the door to the cabin.

"Oh, my goodness!" Andorra Prendergast stepped to one side to allow the other women entry. "It is boarding school again."

The cabin was a disgrace. The bedding was scattered around the floor. Suitcases had been upended and it looked as if the contents had been kicked around the room.

"*Do not touch!*" Celine Cartwright snapped as the women prepared to pick up some of the items scattered around the room.

Everyone froze in place.

"*Someone, grab a mop!*" Celine stepped further into the room, leaving the doorway clear for others to step out and grab supplies from the supply cupboard standing in the corridor. "We can use the mop handle to move items about. We need to check carefully to ensure that we have not been left any nasty surprises."

"This is why I prefer to work with horses," Eugenie Carpenter sighed.

"What are we looking for?" Helen Benson, the mop she had taken from a supply cabinet in hand, stood looking at the mess.

"Moisture." Andorra too had a mop in hand. "We must be sure the lovely young seamen who left this mess for us have not urinated on our belongings and bedding."

Sounds of disgust echoed around the cabin but, rather than be defeated by this visible demonstration of the attitude of the men on this base, the women rolled up their sleeves and prepared to muck in.

Henny stood with her back to the door, watching as the women took control of the situation. With gritted teeth she tried not to show her abject horror at this treatment. What was the point? They were essentially in enemy territory as had been demonstrated more than once since their arrival and until she knew who among the top echelon of this base she could trust, she was powerless.

"Krista," Elaine Greenwood took Krista's elbow, "grab a mattress. We can check each one for any unpleasant surprises. If we get all of the mattresses back on the beds we will at least have cleared the decks and have room to move."

The two women began to remove the first of many mattresses from the floor.

"We need replacement sheets for twenty beds." Celine Cartwright, her green eyes spitting fire, glared at the woman behind the high counter of the base laundry. She put the knotted sheet-wrapped bundle she carried onto the countertop.

Elaine and Krista stepped up and they too put bundles of sheets on the counter.

"Them sheets were put out fresh yesterday. This isn't the Ritz. We don't issue clean bedding on a daily basis, Yer Majesty!" the plump sweating woman snapped. "Talk to the quarter master if you expect special treatment."

"Oh, we have been receiving very special treatment from the moment we arrived." Celine unknotted the cover sheet of her bundle. She had planned for this. "Those are boot marks danced all over the sheet." She held up one of the sheets, clear black marks ground into the white material. "We were fortunate they refrained from relieving their bladders all over our belongings."

Krista and Elaine stood back, waiting to see what would happen. Celine was a sight to behold, her tall figure almost vibrating with her fury.

"They need to be put on report." The laundry woman had heard a great deal of moaning and groaning from the ratings about this group. She didn't agree with them but she kept her mouth shut. She needed this job. She had kids to feed.

"We are sorry for the extra work we are giving you," Krista stepped up to the counter to say. "But we cannot be expected to sleep on dirty sheets."

"I'll change them this once." The laundry woman threw the three bundles onto the floor and kicked them in front of her towards the washing room. She knew the men and women working in the laundry had heard every word but nothing was said as the three bundles were picked up and placed with the dirty laundry.

"Well, that went better than expected." Celine was holding one of three brown-paper-wrapped parcels of sheets tied up with twine.

"We will have to think of a way to protect our cabin when we are not there." Elaine had been warned by her father, the naval captain, to never complain. The rank and file were expected to shut up and take it on the chin "like a man". She no idea how they could protect their belongings. They couldn't post a guard, for goodness' sake.

Krista, her parcel hanging from her fingers, walked behind the two women, looking around at the passing sailors. Was it her imagination or did some of the young men smirk as they passed?

"Do either of you need to go into town with the others?" Celine looked over her shoulder to include Krista in the conversation.

"I have no need of extra clothing," Krista said.

The group had been given the opportunity to travel into Portsmouth on the bus to purchase any articles they needed to improve their appearance as a group of trainee Wrens.

"I too have everything I need," Elaine said. "But, since we have been given passes to leave the base, I am thinking of taking the bus into town with the others. I would prefer to have something to eat off the base when I can. Portsmouth no doubt will have a popular fish and chip shop."

"Capital idea –" Celine began to say when the sound of hurrying feet sounded behind the women.

All three turned swiftly to face the sound – braced for attack.

"Krista!" Perry slowed down and stopped. He strolled over to join them, a smile on his handsome face flashing his twin dimples. The naval uniform flattered his tall broad-shouldered physique.

"Perry." Krista watched him walk towards them. He still had a hitch in his stride, compliments of a horse-riding accident which left him with a weak leg. She turned to her companions. "Ladies, allow me to introduce you to Peregrine Fotheringham Carter, an old friend of mine."

"Ladies." Perry, in full uniform, touched the brim of his cap.

"Perry, meet Celine Cartwright and Elaine Greenwood."

"Charmed." Elaine examined the insignia on the sleeves of the man's uniform. There were several she didn't recognise. She made a mental note of their design, determined to look them up. She had thought she was aware of all naval insignia, thanks to her father's insistence on his children studying such things.

"Any relation to Admiral Sir Henry?" Celine asked.

"My father." Perry shrugged, accustomed to being asked about his relationship to the admiral whenever his name was mentioned. "Krista, I've been told your lot have been given a pass to leave the base." He was aware of the interest they were attracting from sailors walking more than once past their little group. "May I take you to dinner?"

"Will you be in uniform?" Krista had no intention of attracting that much attention by stepping out in a town like Portsmouth with a naval officer, even if she didn't know what all the braid and badges on Perry's uniform meant.

"No." Perry understood her concerns.

"Do you have a car available to you?" Krista knew she would be quizzed by the women later.

Perry laughed. "No, we can either walk or take the bus."

"I would enjoy a good meal eaten in pleasant company." Krista needed to talk to Perry. What in the world was he doing here? Would he be at liberty to tell her?

They made arrangements to meet and, with another brief touch of his cap brim, Perry took his leave of them.

"You sly old fox!" Celine nudged Krista while admiring Perry's rear view. "An admiral's son. Well, well, well."

"How good a friend is he?" Elaine asked. "He is quite the dish."

"Perry is just a friend." Krista blushed when the other two laughed.

Chapter 5

"Perry, what are you doing here?" Krista was wearing the only dress she had brought with her. The flowered navy dress and coat had been packed in case of necessity. She was glad now she'd included the items in her luggage.

They were in the dining room of a small exclusive hotel on the outskirts of Portsmouth. He had not been willing to speak of his affairs while standing waiting for the bus. She had tried again to get him to tell her his business when they were on the single-decker bus but he had refused.

"In this hotel?" Perry, looking elegant in his grey pinstripe suit and impeccable whites, accepted the large leather-bound menu from the white-gloved waiter. "It came highly recommended to me."

"Indeed." Krista accepted her copy of the menu.

"We will summon you when we are ready to order," Perry told the waiter.

He opened the menu, indicating that Krista should do the same with a jerk of his head towards the menu she had placed on the table. "Let us order and then we will speak."

"You are being very mysterious." Krista opened the menu, delighted to note it was printed in French and had some items she recognised as familiar favourites. Did she dare order them and risk being disappointed?

"Ever since our camping adventure I feel as if I have fallen into a Sherlock Holmes novel." Perry appeared to give his attention to the menu but she could see he was carefully examining his fellow diners and the waiting staff. "Why don't you order for us?"

"Really?" Krista used the fingers of one hand to lower the menu from Perry's face. She stared into his amber eyes, brows raised questioningly. Perry was not an adventurous diner as she had discovered on their camping adventure through Belgium and Germany. "You trust me to order?"

"As long as there are no snails or frog-legs on the plate." Perry stared into her startlingly blue eyes, willing her to agree.

"Very well." She returned her attention to the menu. "We are so close to the sea I had thought to order everything fish-related on the menu." She spoke in a bright light tone of voice while her brain scrambled. Surely he did not believe there was danger in this little out-of-the-way place? "I have changed my mind."

Perry lowered his menu after sufficient time had passed for her to study the offerings. "Are you ready to order?"

"Do you enjoy rabbit?" Krista looked over the menu to ask. "There is a rabbit dish on the menu that I wish to order but the menu states the portion size is for two people."

"Fine." He closed the menu.

"Cream of mushroom soup for a starter?" She knew he enjoyed creamed soups.

"My mouth is watering."

He summoned the attentive waiter with a raised hand.

"The lady will order." He passed the menu to the waiter, ignoring his sniff of disapproval. It wasn't the usual thing for a woman to order for her male companion. He almost closed his eyes in pleasure when Krista placed the order in lyrical French before giving her menu to the waiter.

"Perhaps it wasn't such a good idea of mine to invite you to dine." Perry almost sighed as the sommelier approached their table. "We will have more chance to speak when the main meal is served, I think." It was a week night so there were not very many diners. The waiters had time to give their table a great deal more attention than he was comfortable with – he wanted to talk to Krista and this was the only way he could think of, to get her away from the base.

47

He ordered a bottle of red wine after consulting with the sommelier and with Krista, much to the sommelier's horror. The woman was French, for heaven's sake! Who better to discuss wine with?

"You will develop a nervous twitch if you do not relax," Krista said as the serving staff finally left their table. They had enjoyed the cream of mushroom soup but the spoons had barely been laid down on the rims of the empty indented soup plates before waiters appeared to whisk the dishes away and hover over the table.

"We need to discover a place we can meet to speak without eyes and ears on us." Perry cut into his portion of the rabbit dish with his silver knife. "This is not ideal by any means."

"Are you finally going to tell me what you are doing on a navy base – and in naval uniform?" Krista wanted to moan at her first taste of rabbit. It was wonderful and so familiar, just as the soup had been. She could almost imagine herself back in the kitchen of the Auberge du Ville in her home town of Metz.

"I am here for a short time only as an observer. That is not to say I could not have been an excellent professor of Morse code." He smiled widely. "As the son and younger brother of a sailing family I have been using Morse code for as long as I can remember. It is a useful way for a young boy to keep secrets from his tutors and keep his friends amused."

"Really?" Krista wasn't going to be fobbed off with that little information.

"There are talks being held at the highest level, to instate a singular agency to gather information for all arms of the forces. We cannot remain separate services. We must work together but getting the Powers That Be to agree with one another is extremely difficult. Thank goodness it is not my problem to solve. I am merely one of many being sent 'hither and yon' to discover what I might about the mood of the service men and report my findings." He held up a hand when Krista opened her mouth to speak. "I am also tasked with judging the mood of the base with regards to females being introduced into the naval service – my mother had a word in my father's ear."

"And ..." Krista was trying desperately hard not to shovel the food into her mouth and groan aloud with pleasure. It was delicious and she could swear she recognised the flavours and textures. It was wonderful to be able to enjoy fine dining in elegant surroundings. The attitude towards the women from the sailors in the NAAFI was not conducive to food enjoyment. The food too left a great deal to be desired.

"It was also thought – by the Powers That Be – that Portsmouth being a port, perhaps there would be people here who studied and used foreign languages on a regular basis." He looked to one side. "Like our waiter and his knowledge of French."

"Our waiter didn't understand a word I said." Krista laughed. "He knows enough to recognise the items on the menu but that is the extent of his knowledge."

"Are you sure?"

"Very."

"I tried to tell them it was a mistake to send me and others like me out looking for people with language skills who could be conscripted into the services." Perry wanted to hit his head off the table. Krista was far better equipped for such a task than he. It was ridiculous – to his mind – that she was being disregarded because she was female. Attitudes needed to change but it wasn't going to happen today or tomorrow. In the meantime, it was up to him and people like him to do the best they could. It felt like an impossible task.

"You are to scour the country looking for people with language skills?" Krista didn't say how ridiculous she found this. But then, hadn't Gerda mentioned a group of men visiting her neighbourhood in London seeking people with knowledge of the German language? So perhaps there had been some level of success from this endeavour.

"So it would appear."

"Why do the forces not look within their own ranks?" Krista took a bread roll from the basket on the table. Something she had ignored up to this point. She had no wish to spoil her food with bread but now she simply had to use the bread to soak up the sauce on her plate. She opened the roll and removed the centre, sniffing in appreciation of its wonderful aroma. It too was familiar. "Captain Waters is an Army officer. The man speaks three languages fluently as I know from when he examined my own language skills."

"We have a few – a very few – gifted linguists." Perry

copied Krista's movements with the bread roll. The rabbit thing she had ordered was delicious. He hated to waste any of the thick wine-and-herb-rich sauce. "We need many more and have begun to search but it is like looking for a needle in a haystack. We cannot advertise for the men we need – it is all strictly on the down-low at the moment." He used his fork to carry the bread he had soaked in the sauce to his mouth. "We are having a greater level of success in advertising for secretarial staff with language skills. Then, too, we have found young women studying European languages in the hopes of securing positions that will allow them to travel and teach English – much like your own Miss Andrews taught you."

"There is to be a salary offered to the people you seek, one hopes?" Krista could not afford to offer her services for free. She needed to earn a living to survive – most people did she had found.

"A generous remuneration package is to be offered." Perry blotted his lips with his napkin. He'd been nervous about eating the food she had ordered but it had been delicious. She had taught him on their travels together that he needed to open his life to new experiences. "There will also be additional income for each language spoken fluently."

"That is all to the good, Perry. It is about time someone with sense realised that most people cannot simply volunteer their services. Now, if I am not suffering from an over-active imagination I am about to present you with a recruit."

She had seen the trolley set up for the waiters to

produce flaming desserts. They were trained to make a big production of the actual preparation and service. However, there was a certain social cachet in having the chef himself prepare the dessert at the side of the table. There were very few diners left in the restaurant so it should not be too difficult to have the chef leave the kitchen. But she couldn't march in there as she wanted to and demand to see the man.

"What are you up to now?"

"Summon the waiter over – order Crêpe suzette for dessert and ask for the chef to do the honours – you will not be disappointed."

"I couldn't eat another bite." Perry almost groaned.

"Perry – do not be tiresome – just do as I say." She hoped she wasn't wrong but how could she be? She had recognised the flavours of every mouthful they had consumed this evening.

She bit her lip at the reaction of the waiting staff to Perry's request for their Crepe suzette to be prepared at the table by the chef. She watched black-and-white-clad waiting staff buzz frantically around as they prepared a silver service trolley. Mentally humming Rimsky-Korsakov's flight of the bumblebee for her own amusement, she watched citrus fruit being polished until the skin gleamed. A tall silver sugar-shaker and the silver cover for the portable stove that would be used to cook the crêpes were soon gleaming. It was pure theatre. Heaven forfend that something the great man needed should be missing from the trolley.

"Is this your idea of a joke?" Perry asked as their

table appeared to be invaded by uniformed staff bustling about. He wanted to laugh at the theatrical element and the attitude of the serving staff.

"I promise you: if I am right you will have your money's worth." There was a stiff additional charge for having the service performed by the chef personally.

When the doors leading into the kitchen were pushed violently open and a string of abusive French sounded, the waiters formed a respectful line to herald the great man's appearance.

There he stood, attired entirely in white from his toes to the tall chef's hat on his head.

Philippe Dumas.

The man Krista had been raised to think of as her brother.

Oh Lord, what had she done? She had never told Perry or anyone really about her time spent at the Auberge du Ville in Metz as the only daughter of the Dumas family. A family of short, broad-shouldered, dark-haired, dark-eyed males. She was the ugly duckling in the family: a tall, blonde, blue-eyed female. It was Philippe who told her she had no blood relationship to the Dumas family. Why hadn't she thought before she did this ridiculous thing?

"Philippe!" Krista called out as he approached the table.

"*Krista!*" He stopped in his tracks and stared. "Name of the dog! What do you here?" he demanded in French. "Is it you who ordered those stupid crêpes?" He looked around the restaurant, noting the practically empty room. He clapped his hands together loudly and in English ordered the waiters to clear and close the restaurant.

"It was the only way I could think to get you out of your kitchen," she answered in French. She stood and walked slowly towards him, examining him with her eyes. He had aged since she had last seen him and was visibly thinner. They had much to talk about but not in front of an audience. "I was sure I recognised your hand in the preparation of our meal. You always did have a unique way with herbs and spices."

"Do you really want crêpes?" Philippe asked in French.

"No, as I have said, I wanted to see if I was correct and it was you in the kitchen. This was the only way I could think of to get you out here. Come meet my friend." She took his elbow to lead him to the table where Perry sat staring at them.

Philippe held the chair for Krista, giving her ankle a soft kick as he did so. It was a sign she understood. He was telling her to hush.

"I am Jean-Philippe Coutard, *chef extraordinaire!*" He gave the words a French twist. "Who are you?"

Krista had to keep her mouth from dropping open at the name Philippe gave. It would seem she was not the only one with secrets.

"Philippe, allow me to introduce you to my friend Peregrine Fotheringham Carter. Perry, Philippe is a childhood friend of mine."

Chapter 6

"I hate this thing!" Philippe tore the tall white chef's hat from his head, revealing flattened black curls and a sweat-beaded forehead. His brown eyes, with thick black eyelashes and brows that Krista had always envied, glittered.

They were sitting in an alcove off the kitchen reserved for the chef's use, Philippe on one side of the oblong table with Krista and Perry facing him. The kitchen was closed, all of the staff having left for home. The restaurant too was dark. Philippe had carried three glasses and a bottle of his personal stock of red wine to the table.

"Before we catch up on old news, Philippe," Krista kicked his ankle with her toe under the concealment of the table, "tell me, what you are doing here? Are you on a long contract?" She knew from many years of living at the Auberge du Ville that many chefs toured the world, seeking out new recipes and new food experiences. They were primarily young men who dreamed of opening their own restaurants sometime in the future.

"I have a three-month trial period which ends next week – why do you ask?" Philippe wished there was a way to get rid of Krista's friend. They needed to talk. He wanted to know how on earth she had ended up in his restaurant with one of the British upper classes as her companion. Why had she left France?

"Good!" Krista practically clapped her hands. She turned to Perry, grinning with delight. "Perry, you are seeking men who speak several languages fluently. Philippe – I know for a fact – speaks English, French, German and Dutch fluently. He is just what you are looking for!"

"Is he indeed?" Perry consulted his gold wrist watch and frowned. "I really wish to speak with you more on this matter, sir, but first I need the use of a telephone. If I do not telephone and request a late pass for both of us, Krista, we will find ourselves on report."

"Goodness! I hadn't even thought of that." Krista wasn't accustomed to having to have written permission to come and go.

"There will be someone in reception who can help you with an outside telephone line," Philippe said.

"Excuse me while I take care of that." Perry left the kitchen in a hurry.

"Quick, tell me what is going on!" Philippe leaned in to hiss.

"The first thing you need to know is that my name is Lestrange now. Everything else can wait. Tell me, quickly, how did you manage to get Jean-Philippe Coutard's papers? What did it cost you?" She knew Coutard – he was a temperamental chef not known for his generosity.

"When I left the Auberge du Ville I had very little money. I planned to work my way towards England, taking any jobs I could find. I was determined to get as far away from Metz and my family as I could. I met Coutard in Belgium. I made a deal with him – his papers for my recipes – he agreed. It was no skin off my nose. I never intended to be a chef anyway."

Working in a family-run hotel or *auberge*, one had to be ready to lend a hand at any time. You learned a great deal of many different disciplines – Philippe had always preferred the kitchen – he had a great deal of natural talent as a chef.

"Why would Coutard agree to something like that?" Krista asked. "The man is not known for his generosity."

"He needed it to appear as if he had left the country," Philippe leaned in to say. "Should anyone care to check. I wanted to get away. It was a fair trade for both of us." He had no intention of mentioning the underground resistance that was being set up with Coutard or, as he was now known, the wolf –'Le Loup' – as a leading member. "What caused you to leave?" Philippe wanted to change the subject but he needed to know what had caused the woman he would always consider his sister to leave the only home she had ever known.

"Your father offered me to Maurice la Flange ..." The horror of the moment she had heard the man she thought was her father offering her to a young man known for being abusive to females was reflected in her eyes.

"*He did not!*"

"He did – only hours after you had run away – I heard him myself – there can be no mistake."

Philippe opened his mouth to object again.

"I had to get away." She looked over her shoulder. How long did it take to make a telephone call to the naval base? "I want to hear all of your news. I will tell you mine – but not now. We need more time and greater privacy." She leaned across to grab his hand, stopping him from raising his wineglass to his lips. "Listen carefully to me. When Perry comes back agree to go with him. You are in this country on false papers – now is not a good time for foreigners to behave in any way suspiciously – you need to sort out your papers. Perry can help."

"I have already purchased train tickets to London for when I leave here in a week, at the end of my contract." Philippe finished the wine in his glass and reached for the bottle to refill it. "I have plans to seek out some of my countrymen. I need to join the fight that is coming. I cannot be standing over flaming desserts for some chinless wonder while the world burns around me."

"You always have been dramatic." Krista smiled but only for a moment. This was too serious. "I have told no one of my time spent as a member of your family at the Auberge du Ville. Please keep that secret for me – everything else you can and must tell to the people Perry will introduce you to."

"Everything else? I don't know what you are talking about."

"Yes, you do, Philippe. You, more than I, know what was going on in Metz for the last few years. As a female I wasn't part of the unease but I felt it – I saw it – you have to share what you know." She leaned over to lock her blue eyes into his brown ones, trying to force her will on his.

"Well, I managed to get permission for us to stay out past the time stated on our passes."

Neither had noticed Perry approach, they had been too intent on each other. He pulled out his chair, wondering what these two had been whispering about.

"But I'm afraid we will have to leave soon."

"Perry, I have been trying to convince Philippe to listen to your offer." She couldn't worry about things like passes at the moment. Great spy she would make. Perry was right on top of them before she had even heard him, for goodness' sake. "Philippe too is from Metz. He has information that I am sure Captain Waters would love to hear." She couldn't discuss their travels through Germany and Belgium at Waters' command. Honestly – secrets – they were a headache – it was so difficult to remember who should know what!

"I would be interested in speaking with you, chef." Perry looked at the other man intently. Krista had shared her feelings about the situation in France with him. How

59

much more would this man know? "We are pressed for time just now, however. I have ordered a taxi to take us back to the base. Would it be possible to arrange a time for us to speak at length?"

Krista sat back and listened to the two men make arrangements.

"*Here she comes!*"

The whisper sounded loud when Krista, her shoes in hand, tried to sneak back into the women's cabin.

Someone opened the curtains over one of the long windows in the room, allowing the light from outside to carry into the room.

"I was told you would be late getting back." Henny pushed back the bedcovers and grabbed the woollen dressing gown that she'd left at the end of her bed. She needed to keep order.

"I am sorry, Miss Henderson, the delay was unavoidable." Krista made for her bed.

"You are a sly one!" Gerda Mullins accused her. She stood in her flannelette nightgown, her feet bare, hands on her hips. "You are stepping out with an admiral's son. You create a bad image for all of us. You are a fast worker, I will say that for you!"

"*You were seen at the bus stop!*" Alice Newton called from her bed. She didn't need to keep her voice down. No one was asleep. They were all simply agog to know how this young woman had managed to catch the interest of such a well-connected male. "There would be no point in denying anything, you clever puss!"

"Perry ..." Krista was trying to remove her outer wear.

"*Ohhh, Perry!*" came from several voices.

"Peregrine Fotheringham Carter, if you must," Krista was not willing to be interrogated, "is a close family friend of my guardian. He was as surprised to see me here as I was him. We had dinner together – out of uniform – to catch up on our news. I daresay that is the end of it." She would not mention her guardian's name. How much more intrigued would these women be to know that her guardian was sister to Rear Admiral Andrews! She closed her eyes on a sigh. Secrets – how she hated them!

"This is all very intriguing," Celine Cartwright sat up in bed to say. "But I for one wish to get some sleep. We shall be marching around that square out there very early in the morning."

Loud groans greeted her words.

Krista ignored them all. She grabbed her nightclothes and made an escape into the cold bathroom. She hurriedly washed and when she returned to the cabin all the windows were covered. There was just enough light seeping around the curtains to see her way to her bed. She could feel eyes upon her but with a sigh crawled into bed. It had been a very long day.

Perry managed to inform her – while pretending to give her instructions in Morse code of all things – that Philippe refused to leave before his contract was up with the hotel. He wished to protect Coutard as long as possible. But, at the end of the week, he would join Perry and Captain Waters, much to her relief. He would not be safe but he would no longer be someone using false papers.

Krista came in for much teasing because of their whispered conversation but she did not care. She needed to know Philippe would share what she was sure was important knowledge with the right people.

In the days and weeks that followed, Krista's relationship with Perry was forgotten. The fact that Perry disappeared from the base was a source of gossip for a while then also forgotten.

The women were soon busy learning all they were being taught and ignoring the verbal and sometimes physical abuse they suffered from the seamen who resented the very thought of women being allowed to join their august service.

The three 'specials' as Elaine, Krista and Gerda were soon called by the other women were being drilled – more intensely than the others – in Morse code, radio-handling and motorcycle-riding. Andorra Prendergast offered help to all who needed it. Her years as captain of her own yacht proved invaluable in the help she gave to the other women in signalling, sailing terms, navigating and Morse code. Elaine drilled the women in recognising naval insignia. The women became a tightknit group as they helped each other thrive in the new world that was opening to them.

Alice Newton had the bright idea of setting the orders

barked at them by Petty Officer Timmons to music. In the privacy of their cabin with the beds pushed to one side the women practised their marching, legs moving in unison, swinging their arms, turning their heads and bodies on command and keeping time to the music some whistled while they practised and practised.

Timmons never commented but it was obvious he was surprised by their well-practised formations.

So the weeks of training passed with some struggling more than others. The weather changed, the sun stayed longer in the sky and the first group of Wrens were being turned into a force to be reckoned with – at least in their own opinion.

Chapter 7

"Does it not appear to you we pull this duty far more often than any of the stuck-up girls around here?" Gerda was on her hands and knees scrubbing the deck – otherwise known as the floor of their cabin or room. Her moaning tone was perfect for the execution of their plan. The open windows of the room allowed the sailors that always lurked somewhere about to hear the opening act of their little drama.

The three windows in this room had proved a nightmare for the women but were considered an enormous source of entertainment for the ranking seamen. The curtains had to be kept open for light and, in this glorious weather, the windows themselves remained open when the women were in the room. The women were under constant observation and they knew it. They had accepted and to a great extent ignored the abuse they had received at the hands of the ranking seamen but they were leaving and had decided it was time to get a little of their own back.

"That lot are going to be officers." Krista leaned back on her heels to dramatically mop her brow with the sleeve of her blouse. She grimaced over at Gerda, biting her tongue against the urge to remind her that she was extremely gifted at sliding out of any duty that might involve actual work.

"*Are you two not finished yet?*" Andorra ran into the room with an almost panting Eugenie at her heels. "*The dreadful place isn't that large. Do hurry up!*"

"Mind where you walk! What are you doing here?" Krista snapped in her best put-upon tone as planned.

"I have a run in my stockings and I think one of my garters has snapped." Andorra groaned. "This navy business is hell on clothing." She put a foot onto a bed on the opposite side from the three long windows of the room, giving anyone lurking outside those windows a clear view. She hiked her skirt up to reveal long elegant legs shining in silk stockings. "Do check for me, Eugenie," she turned her head to demand, snapping her fingers loudly, repeatedly giving in code the headcount of the sailors gathering outside the windows. She paid close attention to the sailors shouting at their friends to come see the show while almost salivating as they leaned against each of the three windows for a better view of her legs.

Krista and Gerda picked up the scrubbing brushes and returned them to their buckets.

"*Now!*" Andorra yelled.

The six women hiding, one to each side of the long open windows, picked up their buckets and with loud shouts threw the contents over the sailors gathering around each window. They slammed the windows shut, locking them down. Then stood in the windows laughing. There were shaken fists, curses and promises of retribution from the young men who were soaking-wet and angry on the cobbles outside the Wrens' cabin.

Clapping was heard from the room off the dormitory, which had been set aside for the Wrens' use as a lounge.

"Well done, ladies!"

"That was almost as good as a trip to the theatre!"

"Timing is everything." Eugenie stood with her hands on her hips, glaring out the windows at the retreating sailors.

Helen Benson, carrying a mop, walked into the room. "Ladies, if you will return those buckets – and please don't make a mess in the sinks we have just scrubbed until our knuckles bled – I will run the mop over the floor. Quickly, ladies, we do not have much time. Someone give Krista and Gerda a hand getting tidied up."

In the six weeks they had been on the base, the women had lost three more of their number. They had been marched in formation until their feet bled. They studied Morse code, flag signalling, whistle signals, royal naval uniform insignia, ships insignia and the size and shape of the vessels until they sometimes felt as if their brains were going to bleed from their ears. They had learned to tie knots, been shouted at and jeered while learning to march in formation, touched up by sniggering sailors in the NAAFI. They had survived it all.

"What time did Sub-Lieutenant McMasters give for his inspection?" Celine Cartwright carried the empty buckets across the deck.

"Thirty minutes after that lot," Eugenie jerked her chin towards the windows, "got through making whatever mess they had planned. Interesting timing, don't you think?"

The ranking seamen who insisted on hanging around outside their windows had developed the habit of throwing dirt, seaweed and other matter into the women's cabins anytime they were careless enough to leave the windows unattended. It had become wearing on the nerves to have to be constantly alert.

The women firmly believed that the attacks on their person and the constant teams of ranking seamen outside their windows was a planned offensive. They were too controlled to be just random acts.

"It is perhaps not my place to say, ladies," Andorra Prendergast was moving around the cabin at speed, "but I am proud of all of us. That was a very efficient use of Morse code."

"I should never have doubted you." Celine Cartwright had returned from restoring the empty buckets and was lending a hand in assuring everything was shipshape. "I really believed those sailors leering in the windows would recognise the Morse code signals you were tapping out with your finger-snapping."

"Yes, Andorra," Gerda laughed, "all of those hours of extra tuition you have given us really paid off."

"You wanted as many as possible in the line of fire," one of the women remarked while inspecting her bed. "We all knew that from your finger-snapping. It gave me a better understanding of the use of Morse. I, for one, am glad of the extra hours of tuition you offered to us.'

"I don't know why Sub-Lieutenant McMasters is taking this inspection," Andorra remarked as she worked. "Old Henny has been doing a fine job of keeping us all in line. Besides, we don't have a uniform yet and poor old McMasters has a hard time even looking at us in class. He is hardly going to lay hands on us if our clothing is not as it should be."

"I wouldn't object to him laying hands on me," one of the women said, giggling.

"We will have none of that kind of talk!" Celine Cartwright snapped. "Although ... he is rather dishy."

There were muffled giggles to this comment from most of the women. Sub-Lieutenant McMasters had tall, dark and handsome to a tee.

"We need to hurry." Elaine Greenwood was marching along, inspecting the bunks as they had all learned to call their beds. Naval parlance for everything they used had been one of the hardest things to teach this group of women. "Get everything in place and stand by your bunks, ladies. We do not have much time."

There was an organised rush as the women did a

final check of the cabins they had been given for their use. Within moments each woman was standing by her bunk, shoulders back chest out.

Elaine walked along the line of women, examining each and every one. When the women discovered that Elaine's father trained his daughter and sons in naval discipline, they had elected her their unofficial instructor.

"I can find nothing to complain of." Elaine took her place by her bunk. "That, of course, doesn't mean that McMasters won't find something."

"*Officer on the deck!*" Alice Newton shouted.

The door to the cabin was flung open and a bosun's whistle sounded loudly. None of the women moved.

"Fine set of lungs you have, sailor." McMasters gave the sailor standing to attention a sideways look of displeasure. There was no need to deafen people.

"Sir!" the bosun gulped. "*Attention!*" The whistled command was not so loud this time.

The women, already standing to attention, didn't move. Their eyes remained straight ahead.

McMasters marched slowly down the length of the cabin, his eyes missing nothing.

He then turned to march back along the deck. He had heard of the nasty tricks being played on these women but there was nothing he could do about it. Not when the sailors' commanding officers found the whole thing amusing.

"Wrens, you will remain on board ship until given permission to leave. *At ease.*" He heard the movement of feet but didn't look back when he marched out the door. The bosun closed the door softly at his back.

"Well," Mary Black, a soft-spoken woman from Kent, stepped out of line, "what was that all about?"

The door opened again and Hildegard Henderson – Henny – stood there with another woman by her side.

"Wrens, stay where you are."

The two women stepped inside to gasps. They were wearing matching navy-blue uniforms liberally decorated with blue braid.

"Wrens, I am Catherine, Duchess of Argyll," said the woman. "I am your commanding officer." She marched down the long cabin, her strides as efficient as McMasters. "I am pleased to be able to tell you," she looked at each woman as she passed, "that your uniforms have arrived." She was pleased to note that no one squealed or spoke. "You have permission to speak."

"Is what you are wearing the new uniform?" Andorra was the first to speak.

The women had all paid from their own funds to have their uniforms tailored to their measurements and had been eagerly awaiting the arrival of their kit.

"Yes, it is."

The duchess, a tall slim dark-haired woman, looked stunning in the navy-blue uniform. The long line of the double-breasted belted jacket was very flattering. The shorter skirt came to just below the knee. Thick dark stockings worn with leather laced brogues completed the outfit.

"Come, I have ordered tea to be delivered."

The women didn't know how to behave under the

circumstances. They had been schooled in naval behaviour but a regular sailor got his uniform from stores.

"The Purser's office will deliver the uniforms this morning," Henny, looking a darn sight better in her new uniform, stepped forward to say. "We will take tea in our lounge and be at ease. This is a momentous occasion not just for you lot but for all Wrens. We finally have a uniform design. Not everyone will receive their uniform yet but the factories have been given the order to produce in large quantity."

Krista, Elaine and Gerda were not quite sure of their status as regards to a uniform but were delighted for their bunkmates.

"Strange, Green and Mule, please step forward." Henny had, in naval tradition, allowed the women to select or be given nicknames.

"Strange green mule." The duchess glanced at Henny. "Easy to remember, is that deliberate, do you think?"

"I wouldn't be surprised." Henny shrugged.

"You ladies are the women under the command of Rear Admiral Andrews." The duchess examined them, sighing inwardly that they were not suitable to join her Wrens. These three women had impressed McMasters – not an easy feat – but rules were rules.

"Yes, Your Grace," Elaine answered for all.

"You too will have a uniform. Your insignia will be slighter different to denote your special status but you will still – to all intents and purposes – be considered a part of the Wrens. I ask you to always remember to portray yourselves with the dignity I hope you have come to learn here." Catherine's smile hid her worry. These three women would be serving in very difficult circumstances.

"Wrens," Henny said to the listening women, "there are slacks with our uniform but what the duchess and I are wearing will be how you present yourself to public view. We will march in skirts. The most part of us will serve in skirts but those of you who will be working aboard ship will of course wear your slacks."

"Thank goodness!" Andorra said with a laugh.

"Come, ladies, don't be shy!" The duchess smiled. "You may examine our uniforms to your hearts' content – but only when there are no male sailors about!"

"I love the lines." Mary Black knew she would look good in this uniform.

"Pardon me," Eugenie Carpenter stepped forward. "Would I be walking the plank if I asked a duchess and our very efficient officer to quick-march the length of the deck?"

There were gasps from the other women. What on earth was Eugenie thinking of. She was showing them up.

"Ah, yes," Catherine laughed, delighted. "You are a horsewoman, are you not? You judge a horse by its gait." She turned to Henny with a smile. "Shall we?"

The two women walked to the door, turned and then stepped out smartly, arms swinging, feet moving in a quick march down the length of the cabin. They about-faced with beaming smiles to the sound of appreciative applause and whistles.

A knock on the cabin door signalled the arrival of the requested tea. Two of the women accepted the trolley from the able seamen and with thanks closed the door in their faces.

"Bring that into the lounge," the duchess ordered, "where we can speak at our ease."

The women trooped into the lounge. The duchess and Henny removed their jackets, revealing pale-blue shirts.

"Wrens," the duchess began when all had been served with a cup of tea, "when your uniforms arrive there will be no braiding. We do not yet know what rank you will earn. You have all been chosen for your special skills. You know there are three among you who will go on to serve directly under Rear Admiral Andrews. I have no doubt you wish them well. For you others, you were chosen because you are older than raw recruits. You have defied what is considered the norm for us women. You have each been successful in a career other than marriage. You women have chosen to participate in a man's world, be it yacht-racing, horse-racing or motor sports. You participated and succeeded. It is this spirit of valour that we wish you to carry forward to our Wrens."

The women glanced at each other but said nothing.

"The days ahead will be difficult." The duchess looked around. "I know of the difficulties you have faced here. That will give you some indication as to what we Wrens will face in the coming days. We have fought hard to re-establish the Wrens. We will continue to fight because we know," she beat the arm of her chair with a fist, "we *know* that we will provide a vital service in the coming conflict."

"Do you have any idea of how we will serve?" Mary Black asked what every woman there was thinking.

"We have been given permission to employ clerics – secretaries and office staff – cooks, kitchen assistants and servers who will wait on table and clean cabins – all of which the navy considers work fit for women and will allow the service to free up men for active service." The duchess appreciated the disappointment on every face. "We, however," she indicated Henny and herself, "who served in the Great War know that our skills in *all* of Navy life will be much in demand. The men will be needed for active duty. We women will provide all other roles. We cannot, however, push our way forward belligerently at this point. It will soon become apparent that our skills will be needed. We will be ready."

"Why were we sent here?" Kate Wilson, a redhead from Surrey, asked. "Was there really a need for us to train in so many different disciplines?"

"We need women who can lead." The duchess accepted a second cup of tea. "It was considered wise to send you ladies here at this time, to see what is ahead for the women you will lead. There is a difficult task ahead of us all. We will have to be able to put our hands to the pumps. Help out wherever needed. We have tried to give you ladies the skills to do just that."

Chapter 8

"I wonder who the ratings will pick on now that we will no longer be available." Mary Black stripped her bunk for the final time.

"Leave the room as we found it!" Henny ordered.

"You mean with the screws loose and the frames ready to collapse?" Helen Benson laughed.

"Ladies," Krista feeling proud in her smart uniform, wearing the slacks as ordered by Henny, stepped forward, "is anyone intending to go to breakfast at the NAAFI before we leave here?"

"I *am* rather peckish," Eugenie Carpenter had her bunk stripped and her bags packed.

The others laughed. Eugenie was always peckish.

"Why do you ask, Krista?" Andorra was giving a quick visual check to her area. "You are not one for stepping forward unless you have something important to say."

"Petty Officer Carruthers tipped me the wink and I –" Krista had to stop speaking when the women all *oo-aah*ed and laughed. Krista had taken to her motor-pool training with a natural aptitude that delighted their instructor Petty Officer Carruthers.

"I said from the very beginning that you were teacher's pet." Andorra laughed when Krista blushed. "What did our esteemed motor-pool sailor have to say for himself? The man hardly speaks around the rest of us."

"That is because you tease the poor man unmercifully," Elaine said with a laugh.

"Ladies," Krista said, "this is serious. The ratings have planned a series of nasty tricks for our final morning on this base. Our belongings will be unprotected if we take the time to eat before leaving." She looked at Henny. "I think we should leave before breakfast without waiting for the ferry that has been ordered for us." The navy insisted on calling the truck that carried the men between posts as a ferry.

"We can walk to the nearest hotel and have breakfast there before boarding the train to London," Celine Cartwright suggested.

"I had hoped the men had given up on trying to discourage us." Henny sighed. "Very well, ladies, orders have been received." She walked along the deck handing out sealed envelopes. "You will find the final results of your exams in here and your orders."

The women tore the envelopes apart, each curious as to the next step in their journey.

"Andorra, I passed the Morse code test!" Kate Wilson clutched her examinations results to her chest. "I could never have done it without your help. Thank you!" The dot-dot-dashes of Morse had been evil horrors to Kate's ears. She had managed to pass the final test. Her scores were not fabulous but she had passed.

"*Wrens!*" Henny clapped her hands to attract their attention. The bosun's whistle was in its place around her neck but she didn't use it. They had found a tweet on the whistle attracted the attention of the ratings who always appeared to be lingering outside their cabin. "I know what orders have been given. I feared the sailors would have something unpleasant planned. It is always good to have a back-up plan in place – so I ordered three taxis to be waiting for my telephone call in case of necessity. We will have a short window of opportunity here while the men are at breakfast."

"Well done, Henny!" Eugenie cried. "My orders are to travel to Greenwich."

"Most of us will travel to Greenwich to what is hoped will become our WRNS headquarters. Strange, Green, Mule – there are three new motorcycles waiting in the motor pool under the eye of Petty Officer Carruthers. You three will travel to Dover by motorcycle."

"That is why you ordered us three to wear slacks." Gerda felt her mouth drying out. She was not fond of the motorcycles.

"So say your goodbyes and make your way to the motor pool," Henny said.

There was uproar in the room as the other women all tried to say goodbye to the three women who had become very much a part of their group. Each woman fought back tears. Who knew when they would meet again?

With their shoulders back, their suitcases beating against their legs, the three women stepped out of the cabin and onto the cobbles.

"Carruthers told me of a side way to reach the motor pool from here." Krista kept her voice low. There were always ratings loitering around the Wrens' cabin even if you couldn't see them. You could feel them between your shoulder blades.

"If the man was not old enough to be your father, I would think he was romantically interested in you." Elaine too spoke in a low voice.

"He served in the Great War." Krista was keeping an eye on the area around them. She didn't want any unpleasant tricks this morning. "He saw how vital the Wrens were to the war effort." She laughed softly. "He married a Wren. To hear him speak of his wife, the woman is a holy terror."

"I never knew that!" Gerda huffed.

"That's because you run in and out of the motor pool as fast as you can," Elaine said.

"I love the motorcycles and Carruthers knows it," Krista said. "Heads up, ladies! We are almost there. *Quick march!*"

The three women arrived at the motor pool unmolested

to find Carruthers alone in the huge building. He was standing like a proud father by three new despatch-rider motorcycles, their chrome gleaming – not the larger, much heavier motorcycles they had also been trained to ride.

"Wrens!" Carruthers barked. "Let's get you on your way!"

"Just a moment, please, sir." Krista dropped her suitcase to walk slowly around the bikes. She checked each one as she had been taught.

"Would you like a spanner, Strange?" Carruthers asked. "I checked these little beauties myself and everything is shipshape."

"I'll take your word for it, sir." Krista smiled at the older man who had gone out of his way to help the women in his motorcycle classes.

"Right, we need to tie your suitcases on the back. You don't want your goods shifting while you move." He pointed to the leather bags, empty now, that hung down on either side of the rear wheel. "These bags are despatch bags and will be your friends when you carry messages. They will keep the papers dry and in some cases your spare uniform."

Each woman chose a motorcycle and under Carruthers watchful eye tied their suitcase behind the seat.

"Now, I requisitioned these items personally." Carruthers held up one hand to stop the women from mounting their motorcycles. "Come with me but keep an eye and ear peeled for anyone approaching these bikes. They should be safe. The lads under me are a decent lot but you can never be sure." He had been aware of some of the nasty tricks played on the Wrens and wouldn't allow it under his eyes.

The three women followed him to his office. He opened the door and stepped inside, reappearing almost immediately with an armful of leather-strapped objects which he handed out to them.

"What are these?" Krista had seen something like them before. Her friend Perry wore one to support his injured leg.

"We call them puttees. They will protect your uniform trousers from muck. Put them on." Leaving them to strap on the leather protectors that went from their ankles to their knees, he stepped back into his office and returned with three sheepskin-lined leather jackets.

The women almost fell on them in sheer delight. It was cold riding along on a motorcycle as they had discovered.

The final items were safety hats, goggles and gloves.

"Will you get into trouble for giving us these things, sir?" Krista didn't want the older man to suffer for his kindness to them.

"Don't you worry none." Carruthers smiled. "I had Rear Admiral Andrews sign off on the order. I'm safe as houses."

"Thank you, sir!"

The three women came to attention and saluted.

He returned the salute before passing out road maps.

"Get away with you now, safe travels and good luck! I know you don't like the motorcycles, Mule, but you need to get used to them. The journey you are taking today is long enough to learn the feel of the cycle at your leisure with no examining eyes on you. Now off you go!"

He watched the three women mount up with tears in his eyes. They had been good students, never complaining no matter how much they were tested by men who should in his opinion know better. He had taught them everything he knew in the hope that it would keep them safe wherever they travelled. He looked at the clock. Time to get a bite to eat, now that he had delivered the motorcycles in the state they had arrived in. He sighed deeply, shaking his greying head, wondering what the world was coming to. With the roar of the motorcycles like music to his ears, he walked out of his little kingdom.

Elaine pulled ahead of the other two motorcycles and, with the hand-signals they had learned, signalled them to follow her. She turned her motorcycle off the road they were travelling on. The other two fell in behind her without question. They journeyed along farm roads and through villages, slowing as they passed along commercial streets in close formation. Elaine led the way along a narrow street towards the sea they could glimpse ahead of them. After a quick stop to check for traffic, she pulled across a wide road and onto a grass verge bordering the sea. The opposite side of the road was lined with Victorian houses. She stopped her motorcycle and waited for the other two to do the same.

"That is Newhaven!" Elaine, straddling her motorcycle, shouted over the sound of the waves and the seagulls. She pointed back the way they had travelled. "I don't know about you two but my navel is tickling my backbone."

"I beg your pardon?" Krista straddled her motorcycle and removed her gloves. With a grimace of relief, she removed the helmet and safety glasses. She took a deep breath of sea air.

"She means she is very hungry," Gerda supplied in a manner that was becoming a habit.

"Bring your motorcycles over here." Elaine got off her motorcycle and pushed it up onto the grass. She waited until the other two had followed her before speaking again. "We are almost halfway to Dover and I for one want something to eat and drink before we get there. This is a good town to stop in. It has an old fort and was a fortified town at one point. I've been here many times with my family on day trips."

"We have passed through several nice towns and villages," Krista kicked the stand on her motorcycle down, "but I don't think I would feel comfortable parking the motorcycles outside a café while we had something to eat. Did you two notice the looks we were receiving while we travelled?"

"I did not take my eyes off the road," Gerda said.

"I noticed," Elaine said. "But I think that was mostly because Gerda was wobbling all over the place. Honestly, Gerda, my heart was in my mouth for almost every inch of the way. That is one of the other reasons I stopped here." She pointed to a long stretch of silver strand, empty at this early hour of the morning. "You are going to ride along the beach until you feel comfortable on your motorcycle." She held up a hand when Gerda went to object. "You are a danger to all of us until you relax and move with the motorcycle."

"I passed my road test the same as you two!" Gerda protested.

"By the skin of your teeth!" Elaine couldn't give in to Gerda. This was too important. "We were each given a new motorcycle." She threw her arm out at the three motorcycles sitting on the grass. "It seems we will be using them as despatch riders since we have been issued with despatch pouches as pointed out to us by Carruthers. You can't be afraid of these machines any longer, Gerda. You just cannot. I am hoarse shouting encouragement at you from the rear."

"Don't start crying, Gerda!" Krista snapped in German. She had noticed Gerda paid more attention to comments in the German language. "We are not picking on you."

"There are miles of sand there." Elaine pointed at the beach. "Take your suitcase off the back – we will look after it. Then take yourself onto the strand – the wet sand, mind you – and get comfortable with your motorcycle."

"Who are you to tell me what to do?" Gerda huffed.

"The person riding behind you and being endangered by your dangerous riding!" Elaine had had enough of Gerda's sensitive feelings.

"Gerda," Krista was removing the suitcase from Gerda's motorcycle, "Elaine is right and you know it." She almost fell back onto the grass when Gerda pushed past her to take her motorcycle.

"What are we going to do with her?" Elaine said as Gerda inched her machine onto the beach. "How many times have we told her it's more difficult to control the motorcycle when you're going slowly?"

"It can't have helped that every time she got on a motorcycle the sailors shouted *'Jelly on a plate!'*. I had never heard that before." Krista watched Gerda putter down the wet sand.

"It's a children's chant." Elaine tried not to laugh. It was mockingly accurate. "*Jelly on a plate, jelly on a plate, with your wibbly-wobbly, wibbly-wobbly jelly on a plate.*" She pointed at Gerda. "I have been behind her all the way and I thought she was going to wobbly off the plate a hundred times."

"I don't understand her." Krista didn't like to speak of their fellow behind her back but they had to get this sorted before they arrived in Dover. "She seems so timid – afraid of her own shadow – yet she can't be. She applied for this special service."

Just then Gerda took a tumble off her motorcycle. Krista jumped up but Elaine pulled her back down again.

"Leave her alone. She is the only one of us that never took a tumble. If she breaks something we'll find her a doctor in the town. Look at what she's doing. She hasn't even turned off the motor but is sitting there waiting for someone to come rescue her. If she's out in the middle of a cow patty in the dark, who do you think will rescue her?" She waved her hands in the air. "And before you ask what the middle of a cow patty means, it means out in the middle of nowhere on her own. She must learn or give up and go home to her uncle's pawn shop."

"You are being very hard-hearted." Krista had not seen this side of Elaine before.

"I don't want her to fail, I really don't, but she has to take responsibility for herself. We cannot carry her." She turned away from the sight of Gerda sitting there crying. "I don't know what we'll be doing from here on, Krista, but I am desperate to serve my country in some way. It broke my heart when I discovered I couldn't become a Wren because my mother is French. But we have trained with Wrens. We are being entrusted with motorcycles. We have been chosen for something special and I for one do not intend to be sent home with my tail between my legs." She marched off down the strand and, when she reached the still-crying Gerda, nudged her backside with the toe of her shoe.

"Stop being a bloody baby! Your arse is getting wet! Now get up, pick up your bike and learn to control the bloody thing or we are leaving you here and taking the bike without you on to Dover." She put her hands on her hips and glared down at the miserable-looking Gerda. "We will do it. We can ride our own bikes with yours in between us and take a handlebar each – now, where you go from here is up to you." And she walked back towards a startled Krista.

"*You have no right to order me about!*" Gerda shouted at her back. "*Just because your father is a captain!*"

Elaine swivelled on her heels, facing back towards

Gerda. "*I want to succeed!*" she practically screamed to the accompaniment of startled seagulls. "*I want to make my father proud – I will not allow you to hinder my progress. I don't care if I get in trouble for sticking my neck out. I don't care if I am overstepping the mark – we need to pull together, Gerda – starting now.*"

She turned away in disgust as the other woman started weeping again.

"Do you have any money?" she demanded when she reached Krista's side.

"Yes."

"There is a hardware shop on one of the side streets." She smiled at pleasant childhood memories of her father purchasing buckets and spades for her and her brothers there. "I'm going to purchase a flask for myself." She patted one of the leather bags on the side of her motorcycle. "This little beauty is going to carry tea and food for me. I drink a lot of tea and want to have my own supply close to hand. I won't ever again stand in line practically begging every time I want a cup of tea at the bloody NAAFI!" She kicked at the grass.

"You are swearing a lot," Krista said.

"I have been biting my tongue for weeks." Elaine laughed. "I know I have no authority here and I could get into a great deal of trouble but, Lord, it felt good to let rip." She turned her head to look down the strand at Gerda. "She is back up. She must not have injured herself."

"Elaine ..." Krista began.

"No, I am sorry, Krista, but I have had a bellyful of catering to Gerda's sensitivities. She is older than either of us. She had the opportunity to leave when we were training – others did. We cannot carry her. She must stand on her own two feet and that starts with learning to control her bloody motorcycle."

Chapter 9

"That was really tasty." Krista balled up the greaseproof paper that had been wrapped around the fried-egg sandwich she'd eaten and thoroughly enjoyed. "Although it feels mean to sit here enjoying our food while poor Gerda rides back and forth."

"Stop referring to her as poor Gerda." Elaine licked her fingers. Her sausage sandwich had been delicious. "She gets away with murder because people pity her. It is time she grew up."

"Here she comes."

"I will soon be out of petrol." Gerda pushed her motorcycle towards them. "And I am hungry. I want something to eat."

"I wondered when you would think of looking at your fuel gauge." Elaine poured tea into the lid of her new flask. She didn't enjoy being a nasty piece but they needed Gerda to pull herself together. She had been coasting along so far. Whenever any dirty work needed doing, Gerda was missing. "The motorcycle won't need additional fuel if Krista and I pull it between us to Dover."

"You are being mean!" Gerda cried.

"No, I'm really not." Elaine stood up. She couldn't have this conversation lolling in the grass. "I bet your cousins were not allowed to box your ears when you were little. You went crying to your grandmother, didn't you? Well, this is where all of that stops. I watched you carefully during training. You allowed everyone else to carry the can for you. But I refuse to be your crutch." She walked away.

"*She is being so mean to me!*" Gerda wailed.

"No, Gerda," Krista replied in German. "She really isn't. You are older than we are. We should be able to look to you. You cannot expect us to take you by the hand. We three have been chosen for a reason. I'm not sure yet what we were chosen for but I intend to do everything I can to make a success of whatever is asked of me. You can be a contributing part of this little group or stand alone – it is up to you." Krista too walked away.

"*I am hungry!*" Gerda shouted.

"*You're a big girl, Gerda!*" Krista shouted over her shoulder. Then she stopped and turned round. "There is an entire town there. Go get yourself something to eat. And some petrol."

***

"Do you think she'll be back?" Krista was examining the workings of her motorcycle's engine. She loved handling all of the little nuts and bolts that made the machine work. It was a marvel.

Gerda had stormed off in high dungeon to get herself something to eat. She had kept looking back over her shoulder as if unable to believe they weren't willing to cater to her every need. They in turn had pretended not to notice.

"I really don't care." Elaine was polishing the chrome of her bike with a large man's handkerchief.

"She left her luggage here."

"My father always told me you have to be cruel to be kind." Elaine sighed and gazed down the road, looking for the portly figure of Gerda. "We were lucky that we could have this head-on with Gerda where there were no ears to overhear us." She consulted her watch. "She has ten minutes left of the time I gave her. If she does not return, I am – as promised – leaving her case on the grass and taking the motorcycle alongside mine the rest of the way." She prayed she wouldn't have to. The motorbike was the property of the naval service but she wouldn't put it past Gerda to leave it on the sand and cry foul. She had watched her in training – her and Krista both – they were to be a unit and she needed to know she could count on them. Krista had applied herself to everything asked but Gerda – dear goodness, Gerda – if she put as much energy into her assigned tasks as she did evading any and all duties she'd be a marvel. They needed to try and get this sorted before they came under official scrutiny. They only had each other to rely on after all.

Just then the puffing figure of Gerda, carrying what looked like a gallon of petrol, appeared in the distance.

"Looks like she decided to continue the journey with us." Elaine nodded in Gerda's direction.

"I think she is quite capable on that motorcycle when she thinks no one is looking," Krista said. "Earlier when she was riding along the sand I pretended to fix my face and turned my back to her. I was able to watch her, using the mirror in my powder compact."

"Why would someone pretend to be helpless?" Elaine couldn't understand it.

"I don't know but from now on she is on her own." Krista didn't enjoy being taken for a fool.

"I tried to telephone my uncle." Gerda marched past them with her nose in the air. "He refused to accept the charges."

"Why did you not put money in the telephone box?" Krista asked.

"Why should I waste my money when my uncle has plenty?"

Gerda took the spout for the petrol gallon from her pocket and fixed it into place. Removing the top from the petrol tank, she poured in the petrol. "Ha, I bet you thought I didn't know how to do that!"

The other two ignored her, preparing their motorcycles for the journey.

"Are we ready?" Elaine asked.

"Are you not going to ask me if I got something to eat?" Gerda had her suitcase tied back behind her seat, the empty petrol gallon can hanging from a handlebar.

"That is none of my business," Elaine said. "You are an adult and perfectly capable of seeing to your own requirements. Do we have to return that gallon can to the petrol station?"

"Yes." Gerda returned the spout to her pocket.

Neither woman warned her that it would make her slacks stink. She knew that as well as they did.

They set off. Elaine took the lead with Krista behind her. Gerda brought up the rear. Neither woman looked back to check that Gerda was following but they both worried about how they would explain the absence of the motorcycle if she wasn't.

"You women are late."

"Sorry, sir." Elaine removed her gloves then pushed her safety goggles up over the brim of her helmet. "We were not given a time of arrival."

"I am Commander Tate." The tall sailor stood ramrod straight as he glared at the three women straddling motorcycles. "You women will report directly to me." He didn't give them time to react. "A cottage in the village has been acquired for your use. We couldn't lodge you with the seamen." He shoved a map at Elaine. "Get yourselves settled in and cleaned up then report back here."

"Here, sir?" Krista dared to ask. This was the motor pool.

"For the moment – dismissed!"

He walked away, leaving the women staring after him.

"What are we supposed to do with the motorcycles?" Krista looked around but the men there were studiously ignoring them.

"The village is quite a way." Elaine was looking at the map. "Since we haven't been ordered any differently I say we take the motorcycles with us. If that's wrong they can tell us when we return."

The cottage when they found it looked charming. It was one of several sitting on a leafy road. Their cottage was surrounded by a neglected garden but there was a shed to one side where they could store the motorcycles – if they were really for their use only – which seemed strange but theirs not to reason why.

They pushed open a wonky wooden gate with difficulty and wheeled all three bikes into the overgrown garden. Krista winced at the pollen and petals splattering onto the chrome of her motorcycle. They hung their gloves, helmets and safety goggles over the handlebars and left the bikes while they made for the front door of the cottage. They had been informed that the key was over the lintel and so it was.

As soon as they stepped inside the musty cottage, Gerda began barking orders to the other two.

"Those windows need to be opened. We need fresh air in here." She marched along the narrow hallway. "The kitchen must be in the back of the house."

"I suppose we open the windows," Elaine said, amused.

"There are no supplies here!" Gerda's voice came from the back of the house. "One of you check out the situation as far as sleeping is concerned. I will make a list of what we will need from the shops. We might as well make use of the motorcycles while we have them."

The other two opened the windows as ordered and started up the stairs.

"*There are no cleaning supplies here!*" Gerda shouted up the stairs after them.

"*There are three small rooms up here and we have indoor plumbing!*" Elaine shouted back. "*But the beds are bare. The mattresses are standing upright so someone has tried to air them out!*"

"*Yoo-hoo!*" a woman's voice sounded from outside.

A rapping of knuckles against the wooden door was followed by the sound of someone opening it.

Krista and Elaine ran down the stairs to stand with Gerda in the hall.

An older woman stepped into the house, followed closely by two younger women.

"We was told we'd be getting Wrens but no one gave us a date. It didn't make sense to do it out just to let it lie dusty, so we were waiting till we saw the whites of your eyes!"

"Mam," one of the younger women rolled her eyes to the ceiling, "you might introduce yourself after you walk into what is now their place."

"Mercy me!" The mother put a hand to her chest. "I

was that excited to see all of them lovely motorcycles sitting in the garden, I forgot me manners. I'm Mrs Fagin, Mrs Marie Fagin, and these are me two daughters. Well, one is me daughter and one is me daughter-in-law but that makes me no never mind." She had delivered it all without pausing for breath.

"Mrs Fagin," Elaine said, laughing. "I'm breathless. I think I was doing your breathing for you there."

"Me mam doesn't need breath when she gets to talking," a blonde woman stepped forward to say. "I am Franny Fagin and this is Sheila Fagin, the daughter-in-law aforementioned."

The three women laughed.

Elaine took the reins. "I am Elaine Greenwood. This is Krista Lestrange and Gerda Mueller. How do you do?"

"Mercy me, Wrens again!" Marie Fagin shook her head of grey curls. "I haven't seen a Wren since the Great War."

The three women didn't contradict the assumption that they were Wrens. What could they say after all? Wrens was as easy to understand as anything else.

"Now, we was paid by the navy to sort this cottage out," Mrs Fagin said. "We have sheets, towels and whatnot washed and aired for you. My son and his family live in the cottage on your right. Mr Fagin and me live on your left so you are surrounded by us Fagins. If you go about your business we'll have the place ready for you in no time at all."

"We were going to go to the shops for tea and milk," Gerda said.

"You leave all of that to us." Marie Fagin shook her head. "Like I said, we were never given a date to expect you. What could we do? We couldn't put milk, cheese and meat in an empty house. Men!" she bit out through her teeth. "What would you do with them?"

"Perhaps we could carry our suitcases upstairs and choose a bedroom each?" Krista was nervous about keeping the motorcycles out in the open. What if they were meant to leave them at the Dover motor pool?

"Do you mind if we stand out in the garden and watch you drive off?" Sheila Fagin asked. "It will be strange to see women coming and going on dispatch bikes."

"Not at all." Elaine went out to get her suitcase.

"Here, before I forget," Marie Fagin said, "Old Dobbins from down the road wants to know if he can tidy up your garden. The man has been complaining about the state of that garden ever since his old mate Macy died."

"That would be wonderful, thank you," Krista said as she moved towards the door.

The three women were soon back and up the stairs. With their suitcases at their feet, they stood staring at the strange layout of the bedrooms.

"Why are the rooms like this?" Gerda said. "We will have to walk through each bedroom to get to our own rooms."

"That will be awkward. I wish we knew or even had an idea of what we'll be doing," Elaine said. "If we work different shifts, that will affect our comings and goings."

"If no one objects," Krista said, "I will take the front room overlooking the road. We know from experience I am lightest on my feet."

They all laughed, remembering creeping around the large Wren cabin. It soon became a game to guess who was walking about and Krista indeed had the lightest footsteps.

"We will have to make sure that we leave a walkway clear at all times." Elaine looked at the doors cut into the walls separating the three rooms. "Perhaps this was once one big bedroom before being divided into individual rooms. I daresay we will learn to live with it."

They left their suitcases in what would be their rooms. Krista in the front, Elaine in the back and Gerda in the middle room. If they respected each other's space, there should be no problems.

"I would love a wash and something to eat and drink before we go back to see Commander Tate," Elaine said.

"I want a chance to walk out the kinks in my body from sitting on that motorcycle for most of the morning," Krista said. "The journey might have been less than four hours but we have none of us ever been on a motorcycle for such a long time and my legs feel chaffed and rubbery."

"I too have sore legs," Gerda said.

"We should ask at the chemist's for cream for chaffing." Elaine wanted to pull the slacks off her legs and expose her skin to the air. The chaffing was painful.

"*Wrens!*" Mrs Fagin called up the stairs. "*The kettle has boiled. Would you like a cup of tea?*"

"Mrs Fagin, you are a saint!" Elaine ran happily down the stairs.

"My goodness," Gerda stood in the kitchen doorway, "you ladies are miracle-workers How did you get this place cleared in such a short space of time?"

The kitchen table was covered in a pretty oilcloth with all the requirements for tea spread across it. The slate floor gleamed.

"With three pairs of hands to do the work it doesn't take a minute to get things organised," Mrs Fagin demurred.

"And my mam is a slave driver." Franny Fagin walked into the room with a bucket and mop in hand.

"Are you joining us for tea?" Krista asked.

"I don't know if I should." Franny looked at her mother.

"We are all in this together," Krista said. "We would enjoy your company."

So, all six women sat around the kitchen table to enjoy a pot of tea and a good gossip.

Chapter 10

"You are late."

How could one be late when one was not given a time and place to arrive, Krista thought but didn't say.

The three women had arrived at the Dover motor pool to find Commander Tate almost vibrating with anger.

"This is the first and last time you ladies will be late meeting with Rear Admiral Andrews." He turned away and presented a fine rear view to the women, who were still sitting on their motorcycles.

Krista waited to see if the other two would say something. When they remained silent she shouted to his back view. "*What should we do with the motorcycles, sir?*" She wasn't a mind reader.

"*Bring them!*" he barked over his shoulder while walking out of the motor pool. "*Follow my car!*"

The three women turned their motorcycles around and with a muffled roar of engines rolled out of the motor pool. The Commander was standing at the kerb waiting for the official car slowly approaching. He didn't give the driver time to come to a complete stop or exit the vehicle and open the door. He pulled open the rear door himself and jumped into the car. They could see him saying something to the driver but from the look on his face Krista was thankful she couldn't hear the words he used.

The three women fell in behind the car. Krista took the lead. They couldn't travel too close to the car. Their vision was limited by its bulk and, if the driver had to stop suddenly, an accident was sure to occur. Krista gritted her teeth and followed along as carefully as she could. It would have been safer and more polite to tell the women where they were going in case they lost him in traffic. But she had discovered that manners and command didn't necessarily go together.

The driver at least was considerate enough to signal his every move which made it easier to follow him. They arrived at an area some distance from the town. Men were erecting high fences around a castle that sat on the headland.

The driver stopped and spoke with the two men standing guard by what appeared to be a hastily erected guard hut. They waved the car in and then the motorcycles. They were going to a castle?

The driver stopped the car in front of the castle. He was slow to exit the vehicle, giving the women time to catch up with him.

"Leave the motors there." He pointed to an area close to the castle and out of the way of traffic. Then he opened the rear door and stood to attention, saluting as the commander stepped out.

"Do hurry up!" the commander shouted.

The women put their motorcycles on their stands, stepping off. They put their gloves under their arms, their safety goggles on top of their helmets and almost skipped along after his hurrying footsteps. He led them into and out of bends at speed, never looking back to check they were still at his heels. They entered what Krista thought were tunnels. The walls were whitewashed and thick black cables ran along them. The lighting was dim. The only sound was their footsteps and breathless gasps.

The commander stopped finally and with a clenched fist knocked on a wooden door built into the white wall.

"Enter."

The commander stepped inside, coming to attention and saluting the man slowly rising from behind a large desk.

"Strange, Green and Mule, sir," he said as Krista, Elaine and Gerda stepped into the room.

They marched smartly to the desk and stood in a line before it, saluting.

"At ease." The man examined them with cool eyes. He walked around the desk and perched on its rim, directly in front of them.

Krista thought his eyes might be grey. He had a half smile on his lips as he examined the women. She could see his resemblance to her friend and mentor Violet Andrews so guessed his identity before he introduced himself.

"I am Rear Admiral Reginald Andrews." He looked as if he wanted to push away from the desk. He stopped his movement as standing would put him practically in kissing distance of Elaine. She couldn't step back – Commander Tate was standing so close that the toes of his gleaming shoes practically touched her heels.

"Relax for heaven's sake, Tate." Reggie wanted to sigh. He had read the reports on these women. The difficulties they experienced in Portsmouth put the navy to shame. But they were still here which said something for their inner fortitude. "Wait over there, Tate." He waved to the wall by the side of the entry door.

As soon as Tate moved the women took several quick steps back, giving the rear admiral room to move.

"I see you have been given nicknames in true naval tradition. Strange green mule!" He laughed. He was sure people believed he had chosen them for their names which was rubbish. It was pure happenstance but it was easy to remember.

"Strange." He pushed away from the desk and took the step needed to put him in front of Krista. "I knew your mother Lady Constance well." He shook his head of attractively silvering black hair. "I was sorry to hear of her passing." His sister had told him she resembled Constance but he was still taken aback by the obvious mix of both her parents in her appearance. "The baron, your father, was a good man."

Reggie was deliberately mentioning her parent's titles and connections. Tate was a snob and a known gossip. He had been foisted onto Reggie by naval command. He would find a place for him. The man had some skills after all. He could either shape up or ship out. Reggie's plans were too important to be ruined by the resentment of the males serving in the King's Navy. By the intent gleam in Mule's eyes it would appear she too was a snob. Ah well, needs must.

"I never knew them, sir." Krista was aware of the others staring at her. She had never claimed to be related to the nobility. She would have preferred her background had remained just that – in the background.

"Green." Reggie stood in front of the stunning young woman. Who would have believed that old Harry Greenwood could produce a beauty like this? He would have to remember to tease old Harry about the milkman and his missus. "Your father is a captain in the King's Navy."

"Yes, sir." Elaine was proud of her dad. "Captain Harold Greenwood."

"From what I have read, he trained you and your brothers in naval procedures." He had been surprised to read that this young woman had skills usually found in a midshipman. "How did that come about?"

"My father claimed it was to give my mother some peace from our pestering, sir." Elaine didn't smile but her blue eyes twinkled. She had fond memories of her father teaching them to sail, march, tie knots, blow whistles and generally keeping his brood busy while his French wife and her family laughed.

"Mule." He moved to stand in front of Gerda. "You, I believe, are a trained shorthand typist."

"No, sir." Gerda stuck her chin out. "That is Strange."

"Really." Reggie didn't like the look of that chin. The name Mule might be more appropriate than it seemed.

He picked up one of the files from his desk. These women had been investigated intensely. He shook the folder in the air, not opening it. "It says here that you were trained in shorthand and typing."

"It was many years ago, sir." Gerda shrugged. "I have forgotten everything I learned."

"We will soon bring you up to scratch." Reggie put the folder back on the desk top. He would put Mule with Tate. They could out-stubborn each other and knock heads all they liked.

"Strange," he walked along the line, "what would you think of working in these tunnels all of the time?"

Krista drew in a deep breath. He had asked and she would answer. "It would be my definition of Dante's Inferno, sir."

"Green, same question."

"Same answer, sir." Elaine was aware of Commander Tate stiffening at their answers. She could do it if she had to but preferred not.

"Mule, what about you?" Reggie snapped.

"One would be safe down here." Gerda looked around. "Sir."

"At this point in time, ladies, I would invite you to take a seat but it is my understanding that you have been on your motorcycles for most of the morning." He smiled gently. "Your first long motorcycle trip if I am not mistaken. Your, eh, your, er, your ..." he gestured vaguely to his behind.

"Sir." Elaine felt brave. This man wasn't acting like any commanding officer her father had warned her about. If he was open to teasing, she would like to know about it. Nothing ventured nothing gained. "If I might suggest ..." She waited for his nod. "Treat us as ratings. We will not be offended."

"Thank you, Green." Reggie almost laughed. The cheeky young monkey. "You are all wearing what I know are new uniforms. You have been sitting on new saddles. I would imagine your backsides are feeling the pain not to mention your legs?"

"Sir!" Tate objected.

"Tate," Reggie almost sighed, "we will all be working closely together now and in the future. We cannot remain stiffly regimented or we will lose our senses."

"Yes, sir." Tate obviously didn't agree but the rear admiral outranked him.

"Now, ladies, the motorbikes will be your personal vehicles. You will be responsible for their upkeep."

He had made that decision when he read of some of the nasty tricks played on the Wrens in Portsmouth. He would not allow anyone to put sugar in the petrol tanks of new motorcycles. These women would have to be available at a moment's notice and travel under difficult conditions.

"How is your cabin space? Is Mrs Fagin taking care of you?"

"Yes, sir," they answered in unison.

"Your duties for me," he walked around the desk and sat down, "will be many and variable. I cannot give you a list of duties as I have no idea at this point of what might be needed." He stood again. He couldn't feel comfortable sitting in the presence of ladies. "I read in your reports that you have been working on your language skills. Is this true?" He walked around the desk to perch on the rim again.

"Sir," Green answered when he looked in her direction, "Strange has helped me to greatly improve my knowledge of the German language."

"Why not you, Mule?" Reggie asked. "You, as far as I understand it, are almost a native speaker of German, thanks to your German grandmother."

"Sir," Mule answered with almost a glower, "I was too busy improving my own knowledge of French. I understood this was a requirement."

"And how did you improve your knowledge of French?" Reggie really didn't like the cut of this one's jib. Still, she had skills he needed. She could soon be knocked into shape. He would see to it.

"Strange is French, sir," Mule said. "She helped me."

"Strange," Reggie looked at the girl with the white-blonde hair and amazingly blue eyes, seeing her as a person for the first time and not a memory of her dead parents, "I was given to understand that your language skills are impressive." He leaned back on the desk and looked at the women. "Green, your mother is a French native. I believe she taught her children to speak French like natives?"

"Yes, sir." Elaine wasn't going to hide her light under a bushel. She did speak fluent French.

"So, you could be the person to judge how Strange speaks French?" He looked at her enquiringly.

"Sir," Elaine frowned slightly, "it is my understanding that Strange was raised in France – French is her first language."

Krista was uncomfortable listening to this man question her language skills. Surely he knew that she was fluent in three languages. Wasn't that why she was here?

"Mule," Reggie turned his head to ask, "what do you think of the German Strange speaks?"

"It is adequate." Gerda was not going to compliment anyone.

"Only adequate?" Reggie asked. Yes, indeed. This one was fond of sour grapes.

"I am not German, my grandmother was." Gerda again almost forgot to show the rear admiral respect. "Sir!"

"Tate!" Reggie snapped.

Tate stepped forward. "I too have a German grandmother," he said in fluent German. "I spent many happy years visiting her extended family in Germany." He looked at Krista for a response.

"Strange –" Reggie nodded his permission for her to respond. He needed to know just how good this young woman was – he'd had to fight hard to get her under his command.

"You are fortunate to have family in Germany, sir," Krista said in that language. "I lived on the French-German border and grew up speaking both languages. It was a common thing and I didn't realise it was unusual until I came to England. I now realise my great good fortune."

"Her knowledge of German appears to be impressive, sir." Tate unwound enough to nod in Krista's direction.

"We are fortunate, Tate," Reggie wanted to rub his hands together. These women were exactly what he needed. "We have before us three women who are trilingual. That will be a boon to us in the coming months."

"Yes, sir."

"Green, Mule," Reggie snapped, "you were both raised in England. How do you rate Strange in her knowledge of English?"

"Excellent, sir," Elaine said immediately.

"Good," Gerda said when the rear admiral stared at her.

"Strange?" Reggie raised one eyebrow in her direction.

Krista allowed herself to smile. She recognised the glint in the rear admiral's eyes. Miss Andrews too enjoyed putting people on the spot. "I have been assured that I sound," she changed her voice to mimic her friend Peggy Matthews, a Londoner, "'just like your one off the wireless'!"

Reggie laughed. "My sister has taught you well." He was giving information about this woman openly. There was a method in his seeming madness. She looked German, so he wanted it understood that she had connections. The news of these women would be all around the ship in no time. He sighed silently. That was the reason Tate was in the room – his loose tongue would spread the news about these women at the speed of light.

"Miss Andrews is a wonderful woman, sir," Krista said. "She has been everything that is kind to me."

"Yes," Reggie stood, "Violet did say she considers you her ward." He opened his arms widely. He resisted – barely – turning to Tate to tell him to make note. But that was not how the game was played. "Why, we are practically family!"

Chapter 11

One of the benefits of riding a motorcycle, Krista realised that evening, was that you could motor along without speaking. She led the way back to their cottage home while the sky was darkening. It had been a strange day and she was ready for a long sit-down and something to eat.

"Well, we'll never be able to say we missed you arriving." Marie Fagin, carrying a large pot, with a loaf of bread under her arm, entered the cottage almost on their heels. "The noise of them bikes would wake the dead. I brought a pot of rabbit stew for you girls to enjoy."

"Someone has cut a path through the grass for us," Krista said as they followed her into the kitchen. "That was very kind." It made getting the motorcycles inside the garden much easier.

"That was old Dobbins." Marie looked at the exhausted young women. They had been out and about all day. Were they supposed to come home and put something on to eat? Where would they find the time?

Elaine almost fell into a kitchen chair. "Something smells wonderful."

"My rabbit stew will soon buck you up. If I do say so myself." Marie Fagin set a match to one of the burners on the gas cooker. She turned the flame down and set the large pot on top to heat up.

"I cannot eat rabbit." Gerda put a hand to her stomach and grimaced. "I have a very sensitive system."

"Do you so?" Marie Fagin hadn't raised five children without learning a thing or two about one who thinks they are special. "Well now, flower, if you have special food needs, I'm sure you know better than anyone what those are. I daresay you are big enough and bold enough to take care of yourself." She took three white bowls out of a cupboard and put a bowl and spoon in front of each woman.

"Oh, but ..." Gerda was left with her mouth open as Elaine spoke over her.

"Mrs Fagin, arriving home to a prepared meal is a much appreciated blessing."

"It is wonderful," Krista agreed. The smell of the stew had her mouth watering and her stomach rumbling.

Mrs Fagin uncovered the pot and brought it to rest

on an iron stand on the table. She ladled stew into the three bowls.

"Is there a kitty, Mrs Fagin?" Elaine was ignoring the complaining Gerda. "We don't want you to be out of pocket while taking care of three extra mouths to feed."

Mrs Fagin began to cut chunks out of the loaf of bread, putting a thick slice by each bowl. "Well, I'll tell you, girls, I remember the Wrens from the Great War. Those poor maids didn't know if they were coming or going. They never had a minute to call their own. So, when the navy asked me to rent this cottage to three Wrens, why, I just added a little bit extra on so I could see you at least have food in your stomachs. Some of the girls in the Great War, they went into bad health because they never had a decent meal. I wasn't going to let that happen to you lot." She didn't mention the women who had lost their lives at sea while serving. Those poor maids seemed to be forgotten by everyone. But the fisher folk in Dover – they knew – and they remembered.

"We don't expect you to wait on us, Mrs Fagin." Krista took a careworn hand in hers and held on while she stared up at the kind woman. "But I could almost kiss your feet for greeting us with a smile and feeding us. It is very, very, welcome. So, thank you."

"Get away with you." Marie Fagin was pleased to be appreciated. It was more than her own family did for her. She'd be sure to tell them – in great detail – how nice these young maids were.

"This is delicious." Elaine hadn't realised how hungry

she was. They had been running hither and yon all day it seemed. Her legs were shaking. Her rear end was sore and her skin was chaffed. They had not been offered anything to eat or drink today. The last time they had eaten was when they stopped before reaching Dover.

"I suppose I must eat this. I need to keep up my strength," Gerda held up the spoon and examined what was on it when she'd attracted the attention of the others at the table. "I have to report first thing in the morning." She sniffed and seemed to force the food into her mouth. "Unlike some."

"I'll have a pot of tea with you girls," Marie said. "My lot have been fed and are tidying up the kitchen. I didn't have a cup of tea after my meal." She busied herself making tea.

"I have to be out and about early in the morning," Gerda said.

"Yes, so you said." Marie was the only person who responded.

"Mrs Fagin," Krista held up her bowl, "would it be terrible if I asked for more?"

"Me too, please," Elaine said.

"Gerda," Marie Fagin smiled sweetly, "you had better not have any more. If you are delicate like." A less delicate woman she had never seen in her life. "Better get some rest if you have to be out and about in the morning."

"Oh." Gerda looked at the other two receiving extra stew and didn't know what to say or do.

"Get along now. The day is wasting."

Gerda reluctantly stood up and Marie shooed her from the kitchen.

Krista and Elaine were desperately trying not to look at each other. They each knew that if she caught the other's eye she would get a fit of the giggles. Mrs Fagin had put a halt to Gerda's 'poor me' routine.

With one ear listening for Gerda going up the stairs, Mrs Fagin began to serve the tea. "Give her time, girls. She is not stupid. She'll learn. She'll sink or swim and you two will have nothing to do with it." She listened for steps overhead that didn't come.

She hurried out into the hallway and caught Gerda hanging over the bannisters, trying to hear what was being said in the kitchen.

"*Are you too weak to make it up the stairs then, Gerda?*" she called up and laughed softly when she saw a pair of clean heels running up the stairs.

"Mrs Fagin," Elaine said, laughing, "if Krista doesn't get to kiss your feet, can I do it?"

"Oh now," Marie listened to the heavy bumps overhead, "I have raised five children of my own and a slew of others." She sat and spooned sugar into her tea. "I always seemed to have someone's baby under my feet. That one," she jerked her chin towards the ceiling, "has been getting away with murder for years I think. Parents don't do their children any favours sending them out in the world not able to take care of themselves."

"Mrs Fagin," Elaine leaned in to say, "you are an angel sent from heaven. Can we ask your advice, please?"

"First time I was ever called an angel." Marie liked

these two. What she had seen of them. "My husband will be surprised when I tell him." She patted Elaine's hand. "Tell me how you think I can help."

"Three is, I think, not a good number," Krista said gently. "I, for one, do not want to start speaking about a housemate behind her back. This is not a polite thing to do. But I too would welcome any advice you might give us."

"You must be tired, Krista," Elaine said. "Your English is not quite as it should be." She had noticed when Krista became weary her English became stiff and sounded forced.

"Never mind all that," Marie could see that this pair really needed to go to bed and rest as best they could. "Tell me how I might help."

"This is our first day of being alone, so to speak – just the three of us," Elaine said. "We were in a group until this morning and while Gerda could be a pain it didn't seem so difficult when there were more of us." She hated to bad-mouth the other woman but really today had been the giddy limit.

"I do not mean to be unkind about Gerda in any way, but she is an adult who wishes to be treated as a helpless child." Krista didn't want to make an enemy of the other woman but she could not support her through every second of the day. It was more than her nerves could take.

"You must let her sink or swim on her own merits, as I've said before," Marie said. "She is quite a bit older than the pair of you, isn't she?"

The other two shrugged.

"She has a trick of getting her own way while leaving others to pick up the slack," Elaine said. "It is hard to explain."

"For example," Krista said, "before leaving the base we two washed our motorcycles, filled up the petrol tank, and checked the tires, oil and water. Our work and our care of the motorcycles will be under examination. We are being entrusted with these motorcycles. Gerda just sat and watched us work. I just know that in the morning – since she has to leave before us – one of our bikes will be missing."

"Do you think so?" Marie Fagin laughed. "Well, we can soon put a spoke in her wheel so to speak. I'll get my Ronny to remove the front wheels of your motorcycles. He does it all the time to his own when he travels into town. It prevents theft, don't you know."

"What a marvellous idea!" Krista almost clapped her hands in glee. "I can do that. It should not prove too difficult a task and I would like to learn. We were going to check out the shed and see if it was suitable for storing the motorcycles overnight. Gerda's is sitting out front waiting for us to move it."

"Are you sure?" Marie asked. "It wouldn't take my Ronny but a moment to shift the wheels."

"Thank you, no." Krista smiled. "I can do it. It will be good practice and I will enjoy it."

"I'll clean up here while you take care of the motorcycles, Krista." Elaine pushed away from the table. "Is that an equal division of labour, do you think?"

"There's a flashlight in that bottom cupboard."

Marie pointed. "I'll leave you girls to it." She rose to leave. "If I might make a suggestion?"

They gave her their complete attention.

"Take the front wheels of the motors up to bed with you."

"Mrs Fagin, you are delightfully devious." Elaine began to scrub the stew pot, laughing. "I would never have thought of that."

Marie waited until her pot was washed and dried before taking her leave of the two women with a smile. She was going to enjoy having these girls for neighbours.

"I'd better leave while my head will still fit through the door."

"Meaning?" Krista asked.

"We have given her so many compliments her head has swollen," Elaine answered absentmindedly.

"I feel really mean," Krista said.

"I don't!" Elaine snapped.

The two women were standing in front of Krista's bedroom window. The room was at the front of the cottage, overlooking the garden and road. They were watching Gerda tear down the road. She was leaning over her motorcycle for increased speed. She was late.

"That motorcycle will fail inspection." Krista shook her head sadly.

"She was quite willing to allow one of us to fail," Elaine said. "Did you not hear her shouts and curses when she discovered our motors missing their front wheels?"

"I hope she didn't damage them. But she didn't seem

to spend any time in the shed. I was watching."

"This morning's charade was the worst case of sheer ignorance I have ever experienced in my life." Elaine shook her head sadly. "We three have to live together in this cottage. We have to work to get along or we will be miserable. Gerda made more noise than a herd of elephants getting out of bed this morning. She knew we two were still sleeping. She made no effort to be quiet. And the noise she made in the kitchen which is directly under my head! I'll be surprised if there is a cup left unbroken. We have to start as we mean to go on, Krista. I don't like it. I'm not enjoying it but I will be danged if I will let Gerda walk all over me. She has to be made to see that her attitude needs to change and the only way we can do that is by showing her. God knows words don't seem to work."

"Miss Henderson did try." Krista had seen the woman take Gerda to one side on more than one occasion.

"Well, shall we venture forth and see what sort of mess Gerda has left for us?" Elaine went back into her own room to fetch a jumper. It was a bit chilly to be walking around in just pyjamas.

"She outsmarted us, girls." Mrs Fagin was waiting for them when they came downstairs. "She let out the air in your back tires." She waved a hand when the other two gasped in horror. "It's alright, my Ronny has a pump."

"What are we to do?" Krista sat down on a stair.

"If she would put as much effort into getting along as she does into being disagreeable, she would be the most popular woman in the world." Elaine sat beside Krista on the stair.

"You two look like a pair of children waiting for Santa Claus." Mrs Fagin said.

"What else did she do?" Elaine had heard the noise.

"Nothing too damaging, but this stops now." Marie wanted to box Gerda's ears. There was no need for this nastiness. "Since she left first this morning, would I be right in thinking she will arrive back here first?"

"We don't really know but it seems possible," Elaine said.

"Right, leave it to me. I'll have a word in her ear and if that doesn't work – well, it won't be the first time I've boxed someone's ears. This is my property and she has no right to damage it or anything in it." Marie jerked her head in agreement with herself. That young madam would find out it wasn't worth getting on the wrong side of Marie Fagin.

Chapter 12

"*Why do I have to ...*"

The whine. It went through Krista's head. She was beginning to hear those words in her sleep. The last month of living in the cottage had been underlined by what felt like an almost hourly battle to make Gerda accept responsibility for herself.

Even Mrs Fagin had thrown up her hands in despair. She had, as she put it, lectured Gerda until she was blue in the face, all to no avail.

"You don't *have* to do anything!" Elaine snapped at Gerda. "We thought it would be polite to inform you that we won't be here for several days so you can do as your heart desires." She and Krista had been out every day, exploring and providing detailed mapping of the coastal roads around Dover Castle. Now Reggie wanted them to travel further afield – a distance that would make returning to the cottage nightly an impossibility.

"But why do I have to ..."

Krista spoke over Gerda's whine. "Elaine, I asked Mrs Fagin's 'my Ronny' about a supply shop for the local fishermen." The women found Mrs Fagin's almost constant reference to her only son as "my Ronny" hilarious. The poor man was surrounded by females. Now they too referred to the helpful man as 'my Ronny'. "I am going to purchase oil-proof clothing. If you want to come with me, we need to leave after breakfast."

The three women were in the kitchen. It was early morning and Gerda was demanding the other two cater to her as she needed to leave first. She was working at Dover Castle in the secretarial pool, refreshing her knowledge of shorthand and typing. To hear her tell it, her supervisor the dreaded Miss March had it in for her. All of Krista and Elaine's sympathy was with Miss March.

"I need to catch the bus." Gerda sat at the kitchen table, a used mug and plate in front of her. She refused to ride the motorcycle every morning, having discovered – thanks to 'my Ronny' – that a bus left the end of the road and passed Dover Castle. She was out every morning in time to catch the bus, leaving her dirty dishes for the other two to clear and clean. The skirted Wrens uniform she wore gave her a certain cachet among her fellow travellers.

"Well, then you need to get a move on." Elaine

shook the empty kettle and almost groaned. Could Gerda not have filled the kettle and boiled it? What had she been doing since she got out of bed? She filled the kettle. She was gasping.

She began to look for the large pots they used to heat the water for their bathing requirements. "Has anyone seen the big pots we use to heat water?" she asked with her head stuck in a cupboard.

"I had to carry them upstairs all by myself," Gerda said. "I could have burned myself."

Elaine left her head in the cupboard. What was the use of screaming at the other woman? They had tried that. They had tried sitting her down and talking to her. Nothing seemed to work.

"You put too much water in the kettle!" Gerda snapped. "It won't be boiled before I have to leave. I wanted more tea."

"Gerda," Krista said through her teeth, "get off your arse and make your own tea."

"I don't have time." Gerda couldn't understand why everyone was so mean to her. "I have a bus to catch. I can't be late or Miss Marsh will be on my case all day. That woman just looks for reasons to complain about me. It's not fair."

Elaine looked at the clock they kept on the kitchen wall. "Then you'll have to get a cup of tea at the NAAFI because you *are* going to miss the bus if you don't budge."

"*That's not fair!*" Gerda whined. "I haven't had enough to eat or drink. Why do I have to –"?

"*Gerda, go!*" Krista shouted in an effort to save the

other woman's life. Elaine looked fit to kill.

She left the kitchen and ran up the stairs to fetch the pots they needed. She tried not to scream when she found the mess in the bathroom. Was it really that difficult to pick up after yourself?

"*It's not fair!*" Gerda stomped through the hallway and out the front door.

On the road she marched along, head up, shoulders back aware of the admiring glances she was receiving from behind lace curtains. The uniform she wore seemed to inspire admiration in others. She had never felt so attractive in her life. She'd discovered a wonderful shampoo in Krista's bedroom. She used it almost every day. It gave her hair such shine and bounce. The pale-yellow towel she'd found in Elaine's room was so soft against her skin. She loved pretty things – why shouldn't she have them? It was so unfair.

She stood in the bus line, ignoring the people around her, mentally composing the letter of complaint she would type up as soon as she reached her desk. Why should she have to go into some dreadful office every day when the other two got to swan around the country enjoying themselves?

"She can move with speed when she has to," Elaine said when Krista returned to the kitchen. She dropped into a kitchen chair. She put her elbows on the table. With her hands holding her head up, she stared at Krista. "We cannot continue like this."

"What can we do?" Krista began filling the large pots with water. She put the pots on the gas stove to heat. With the kettle that had just come to the boil in her hand she turned to Elaine and with a grin the women chanted in chorus "*It's not fair!*"

"If we were just three women sharing a cottage we could ask Gerda to move out." Elaine began to slice yesterday's bread to make toast.

"I don't understand how one person can make such a mess." Krista made the tea in the metal teapot and put it on a low gas burner to brew. "From listening to her speak – do you get the impression she is accustomed to household staff?"

"Krista, even if she lived like a duchess in the past, times have changed for her – for all of us – and we have to learn to deal with it." Elaine thought Krista was too kind to Gerda who took advantage.

"I am truly at the end of my rope." Krista began to set the table while Elaine made toast. "The bathroom upstairs is in a mess – as it is any morning we leave the house after her. She doesn't even pick up her own towels." She grimaced. "Sorry, I think it is your towel. The one you were missing."

"She does appear very partial to our belongings. I think she searches the house when we are not here and helps herself to whatever pleases her. I find her behaviour very strange – frightening in some ways. I simply cannot trust the woman and that is not good." She carried the toast to the table. "Well, we've told her we won't be here for several days. We will have to put our belongings under lock and key which is very disagreeable. Still, one good thing. She will have to pick up after her own lazy arse."

"Are you coming with me to get waterproof clothing?" Krista asked when both women were seated and enjoying tea and toast.

"Has Reggie given you some chits to cover the cost? I don't have a lot of spare cash."

The two women had been asked to address and refer to Rear Admiral Andrews as Reggie.

"He has." Krista smiled widely.

"So, you finally convinced the man that we needed special gear." Elaine laughed. Krista had been rabbiting on about waterproof clothing and whatnot for weeks.

"I love the work we've been doing, collecting all this information." Krista looked over her shoulders automatically to check no one was in hearing distance. "But it makes sense for us to remain outdoors. We are losing time coming back to the cottage every night."

"But camping ..." Elaine almost whined.

"We can't be searching for lodgings, Elaine. Reggie wants what we are doing to remain a secret. If we have landladies and people watching our comings and goings we might as well place an advertisement in the newspapers. Sorry, I think camping is the only way."

"I suppose. Thank goodness for the motorcycles. We would never have been able to get half as much done if we had to rely on public transport. Not to mention your skill and speed at shorthand. That has really been a blessing. I sometimes feel like a spare part."

"Your knowledge of the sea and tides has been all-important, Elaine, and you know it." Krista said. "Stop fishing for compliments."

A loud knocking on the cottage door caused both women to jump. Mrs Fagin and 'my Ronny' knocked first, opened the door, stuck their heads in the doorway and shouted when they came by. No one else visited them here.

They both stood to go and answer the door. You couldn't be too careful.

"Ladies!"

Rear Admiral Andrews himself stood on their doorstep. The man was impressive. Even wearing civilian clothing of dress slacks and short-sleeved shirt, he held himself like a man in uniform. The two women, wearing their pyjamas and cardigans, felt like orphans of the storm in his august presence.

"Do come in," Krista held the door open.

"Good woman," Reggie said softly as he passed her. "You never addressed me by my name or rank. You are learning. The kitchen is this way?" He didn't think secrecy was necessary here but one could never be too careful in these troubled times. He walked down the hall without waiting for an answer, the two women hurrying after him.

"I'm in time for tea, I see." He took a seat at the kitchen table.

"Would you like some toast?" Elaine asked while Krista started a fresh pot of tea.

"Yes, please." Reggie watched the two women work.

Even in these circumstances they worked well together – no wasted movement.

When they were all seated around the kitchen table with fresh tea and a stack of toast sitting close to hand, Reggie said: "Strange, Green, I am pleased with you." He slapped the tabletop. "I didn't think I would be, mind. But I hoped. The work you two have carried out for me in the last month has been first class. Mule, however," he shook his head, "I am sorry to say that Mule will receive her walking papers this evening. A dishonourable discharge is to be served on her."

He waited for the women to speak. They had never uttered a word of complaint against their shipmate. Not in his hearing.

"I have had Commander Tate working with Mule." Reggie hadn't wanted to accept defeat so had tried to give the woman a chance. "He is most unhappy with her work." He looked at the two young women at the table with him, "or should I say lack of work."

Krista and Elaine refused to comment.

"Did you know that she has lodged a total of eight official complaints against the pair of you?"

"Reggie, what do you want us to say?" Elaine asked. "We have tried with that woman. Lord knows we have tried. If Krista bent any further back trying to help her, I was afraid her spine was going to crack."

"I can only imagine. It is a shame because she has the skills I need. She just refuses to use them."

Krista and Elaine sat waiting to see what would happen next.

"As for you two ... Krista, are you sure about sleeping out under the stars?" Reggie hadn't wanted to put the women under his command into danger but things were heating up. Soon every man, woman and child on this island would be in danger.

"Reggie ..." Krista stood and walked over to the windows to check for anyone who might be lingering in the garden. Dobbins came by often to take care of the lawn and flowers. The garden was deserted.

"We have some idea," Krista said when she was seated once more. "of the need for the information you have had us gather. We have mapped what feels like every dent and nick in the coastline for miles around. We have taken readings of ocean tides from rock faces. We have stood on cliffs and stared at the French coastline making note of all activity until our eyes have almost bled. Now you want us to go out with antenna and radio-wave receivers. And while doing all of this we are not to attract attention to ourselves."

Krista waited to see if he would say anything. When he didn't, she continued.

"Your plan as you explained it to us – is to have teams mapping the British coastline."

"You two have been doing a bang-up job of checking sights of interest to me in this area." Reggie said. "It is just – you are females – I did not think of the demands of staying out overnight to collect information."

"It is not efficient for us to leave here each day and return in the evening. If we stay out – under the stars – as you call it, we can amass more information. We will need to retain this cottage – please. We need to wash ourselves and our clothing from time to time and we can report back on our findings. This cottage can be our base of operations."

"I am having a telephone put into the cottage," Reggie said as if he hadn't heard what Krista had been saying. "You may use it for your private needs – always remembering that the operator can listen in – but it will be useful for me to telephone you both and arrange meetings. When you are out and about, you will carry a radio with you. You have been trained in its use?"

"Yes, we have," they both said.

"I am grateful, ladies, for all the information you have been gathering for me. I am awaiting permission for more aides over a greater distance. The work you have done will be instrumental in getting me that permission."

"Reggie," Krista wasn't comfortable addressing this man in this fashion but he had insisted, "have you thought of supplying campervans to the people you send out instead of motorcycles?"

"No." Reggie sat back in his chair. "More tea, please, Green, while Strange tells us about this idea."

Elaine jumped up. She put the half-full kettle back on to boil. The kitchen was getting steamed up and it didn't look as if Reggie would be leaving any time soon. She turned off the heat under the pots of water with an inward sigh.

"If you had several campervans and didn't expect your people to sleep in them, you could have between six and eight people to each campervan," Krista said.

"They could put up tents around the campervan. They could store equipment under it. They would have toilets and kitchens available to them. They could stay out longer and travel further." Krista knew what she was talking about.

"You travelled through Europe in one such van, didn't you?" Reggie had read this young woman's report of her travels through Belgium and Germany.

"So that's how you know about waterproof clothing and folding shovels and cook pots!" Elaine said as she made the tea. "How fascinating!"

"You have never told your companion about your travels?" Reggie was impressed.

"I wasn't given permission to discuss the matter." Krista never knew what she could or couldn't say about her attempts at spying so she played safe and said nothing.

"Krista, you dark horse, you!" Elaine was back at the table, having left the tea to brew.

"I know nothing about campervans," Reggie said.

"You might contact Captain Winters," Krista suggested. "I understood the van we used was his personal property. I do know Perry was terribly impressed by the van and often referred to it as a super little ship on wheels."

"That would be Peregrine Fotheringham-Carter, Admiral Sir Henry Fotheringham-Carter's youngest son?"

"That would be your man."

"Thank you. I will look into the matter."

TO BE CONTINUED

Made in the USA
Middletown, DE
28 July 2025

11338724R00076